Quinn stood at the podium in front of a sea of reporters, cameras rolling, with a patience she couldn't believe he possessed.

But the Playboy Prince wasn't smiling. Not joking. Not charming them into letting him get away with murder.

"Today I want to speak to you about my wife, Dr. Anais Hayes—or, as she's been known since returning to Corrachlean, Dr. Anna Kincaid."

Her anxiety beast reared up in her belly and started chewing.

"Oh, sweet mercy, don't do this, Quinn," Anais whispered.

"What's he doing?" her mom asked, the question also whispered.

"We've never had a divorce, and we're not going to have one now. I'm asking you to give us the space we need to fit our lives back together. I'll do whatever I need to protect her. I came home to fulfill my duty to my family, and she is *my family, so I'm starting with my wife. If we have to leave Corrachlean to have any kind of peace together, to have the family we were always meant to have, we'll leave. I don't want that to happen."*

"Did he just threaten to abdicate?" her mom asked.

"He's not going to be King…" Anais murmured, even though she'd heard his intention clearly. "He can't abdicate, but I think maybe he's threatened to renounce his title."

Why in the name of heaven would he do that?

He seemed done talking, and once again stood stoically for the cameras, waiting.

Then the questions began…

Dear Reader,

I am fascinated by the concept of royalty—even if it also kind of horrifies me. (I'm American—sorry!) I love the drama, the history, the pageantry… And I also kind of hate myself for it.

This is probably something to do with the reason why my royalty stories always end up involving duty versus desire concepts. It's my duty as an American to see the world as 'everyone is created equal'—and I do—but I also desire the fairytale. What can you do?

This book is probably one of the hardest I've ever written, because I had to put it down in the middle to write a different book, then go back to this one… And then pretty much rewrite it. A couple of times. But sometimes characters won't let you go, and I couldn't put Quinn and Anais away without finishing their story.

Actually, even after finishing I'm having a hard time letting go. Quinn's still talking to me louder than my new hero. And let me say—even though I know it makes me sound insane—I'm sort of hoping he moves out of my head and into the reader's head soon, so Gabriel (my new hero) has a chance. If Quinn shows up on your mental doorstep, good luck! He's housetrained, but a bit of a handful…

Amalie xo

AmalieBerlin.com/Contact

Facebook.com/AuthorAmalie

THE PRINCE'S CINDERELLA BRIDE

BY
AMALIE BERLIN

Published in Great Britain 2017
By Mills & Boon, an imprint of HarperCollins*Publishers*
1 London Bridge Street, London, SE1 9GF

© 2017 Amalie Berlin

ISBN: 978-0-263-06979-2

Our policy is to use papers that are natural, renewable and recyclable
products and made from wood grown in sustainable forests. The logging
and manufacturing processes conform to the legal environmental
regulations of the country of origin.

Printed and bound in Great Britain
by CPI Antony Rowe, Chippenham, Wiltshire

Amalie Berlin lives with her family and her critters in Southern Ohio, and writes quirky and independent characters for Mills & Boon Medical Romance. She likes to buck expectations with unusual settings and situations, and believes humour can be used powerfully to illuminate the truth—especially when juxtaposed against intense emotions. Love is stronger and more satisfying when your partner can make you laugh through the times when you don't have the luxury of tears.

Books by Amalie Berlin

Mills & Boon Medical Romance

Hot Latin Docs

Dante's Shock Proposal

Desert Prince Docs

Challenging the Doctor Sheikh

The Hollywood Hills Clinic

Taming Hollywood's Ultimate Playboy

Return of Dr Irresistible
Breaking Her No-Dating Rule
Surgeons, Rivals...Lovers
Falling for Her Reluctant Sheikh

Visit the Author Profile page
at millsandboon.co.uk for more titles.

Hina Tabassum:
Your enthusiasm for my books is something I return to on hard days. Thank you for that. And for your smart reviews. Always a good day when one pops up!

Laura McCallen: Thank you for two years of hard work, dedication and enthusiasm. You will be missed.

**Praise for
Amalie Berlin**

CHAPTER ONE

IT WAS A strange sort of medical facility, but the changes made to Almsford Castle since ex-Princess Anais Corlow's last visit made it seem almost like a new place. Or at least like an alternate version of reality that she could pretend she'd never been to, and never run away from...

Sometimes for several seconds at a time.

Dr. Anna Kincaid—as she was now known—checked her watch. Twenty minutes left in her lunch hour, right on schedule. She climbed onto the gym's treadmill closest to the exit. She could run for fifteen minutes, shower like lightning, and be back in time for her first patient of the afternoon, same as yesterday.

As soon as she got the belt moving, she increased the speed until she had to push herself to keep up. Not a sensible way to exercise but, no matter how determined she was to remain in the new job that allowed her to stay in Corrachlean with her mother and the quiet life they'd built, every minute she was at Almsford she felt the need to run. It built over the day, faster when she wasn't busy helping patients than when she sat alone in her office with just her memories.

Anais had more or less died the moment she'd left Prince Charming, Quinton Corlow, second son of Corrachlean. Without her husband, she'd had no title—something she'd never cared to have anyway—but she'd also lost her country, her home, for the last seven years.

Almsford Rehabilitation Center now belonged to Corrachlean's soldiers, people who wanted her there. People who welcomed her, maybe in even greater proportion to how unwelcome she'd been the last time around. The people made it possible for her to set foot in the grounds. The physical changes to the building made it possible for her to stay, but running in one place kept her from running away.

Protective sheeting covered the stained-glass window running along the top half of the twenty-foot western wall in the ballroom-turned-gymnasium, adding another little barrier to her past, to keep those soul-crushing memories from overwhelming her.

To let her—almost—put it all away.

Laughter, warm and masculine, danced up the corridor that branched off the gymnasium to the first-floor patient rooms.

A sparkling sensation, like the meeting of a million tiny kisses, sprung to life at the top of her head and spilled in a cascade down her back, tickling across her neck and over her shoulders, all the way to her thighs, effectively wiping every thought from her head.

Everything but the thrill, everything but the smile she felt over the thrum of her muscles and the murmur of the machine.

Somewhere inside, part of her soul sat up, and a surge of excitement blossomed in her belly. Images of silk sheets and a field of daisies filled her mind, the brush of green leaves tickled her bare calves as she half ran, half danced through them...

She knew that laugh.

Oh, God.

She stumbled and would've fallen off the treadmill if not for the safety bars.

Not him. Not here.

She wrenched herself from the machine and careened backwards, her legs boneless and quaking.

Quinn's voice came from some distance away, but he might've been walking down the corridor towards her. She could poke her head out to check and smack straight into those famed dimples.

Which way? Gardens?

Too exposed.

How awkward would it be if Corrachlean's beloved, rascally soldier Prince came waltzing down the hallway and saw her there after seven years of self-imposed exile? She'd done her best to change her appearance, even beyond the ways the world and their divorce had changed her. Maybe he wouldn't recognize her, at least long enough for her to skirt past him?

The patients hadn't recognized her, and she'd stayed away from anyone who'd known her except for Mom.

He wasn't supposed to even be in the country—the last she'd heard he was still on tour. At the very least, he should be in another country, castle, the palace or somewhere, with a svelte model on his arm, if gossip rags were to be believed... And why wouldn't they be? They'd been right about their marriage spiraling down the drain, no matter how painful and horrible it had been for them to publicize it in increasingly callous ways.

She'd been back four weeks. It might be a small island nation, but she should've been able to avoid him for a year at least. But one month? Four weeks? Thirty measly days?

Anna shouldn't have any feelings about Prince Captain Quinton Corlow one way or another. Maybe—if she followed the pattern of most of the heterosexual women who encountered the caramel-haired devil—she should swoon at his movie-star looks if he happened by. Swooning involved paling, so that could seem legit.

But she definitely should not be breaking out in a cold sweat and considering whether her heart rate had reached a fast enough pace to require cardioversion.

Before she could muster the courage for a mad dash to

her office, another blast of his voice ricocheted up the corridor, cutting escape from her mind.

Not laughter.

Not words spoken with joy. His voice trembled with alarm and the hoarse expletive that followed either shook her or the building.

A breath later came a terrible bellow for help.

"Quinn..."

Her heart lurched, and by the time her thoughts caught up with her body she was running again, down the long hallway.

He'd sounded far away, but she couldn't tell how far. As she pounded past each open door, she slowed down to peek inside for signs of distress, then spent time dodging people as they limped and rolled out of their rooms.

The residents turned further down the hallway, and she relied on their reactions to direct her.

Three rooms from the far end on the right-hand side, a door stood open and people were gathering around it, forcing her to wiggle through.

"Sorry. Sorry..." she said in passing, and didn't stop until she was through the door.

Even from behind, even despite the changes seven years as a soldier had made to the breadth of his shoulders, every atom in her body recognized him, crouched over someone on the floor.

Her Quinn. Her husband.

No. Once, maybe. Not anymore. As she absorbed his presence, the rest of the room came into focus.

The bed sat upended and had a raggedly cut bed sheet tied to the bars of the headboard.

Hanging.

She moved around Quinn and crouched over the patient on the floor. His skin was still tinged cyanotic.

"Lieutenant Nettle?" She said his name and reached to

check the pulse of his carotid, narrowing her focus to the most urgent place: her patient, not her ex-husband.

Before she could count ten seconds, a large hand clamped onto her wrist, yanking her gaze from her watch's face to Quinn's.

The shock of recognition blazed across his heartbreakingly handsome features, made only more devastating by the years that had passed. His caramel hair, once short and smart, had begun to grow out, but it was his stormy gray eyes that slapped her like an accusation.

She forced her gaze away, down at the patient, mentally scrambling for what she should be doing.

"Don't." She said the only word she could wrench from her mind and, seeing pink returning to Nettle's face, pulled her arm away and stood back up. "I want him off the floor."

"I want his neck stabilized first," Quinn bit back, but the incredulous way he looked at her said he was having as hard a time navigating this sudden overlap of two realities as she was.

But he was handling it better. Of course Nettle should be stabilized first. "I'll…I'll get a brace."

In contrast to the way her body had responded to his laughter, what dug its talons into her now was far darker even than that rise of panic that had bid her run.

Guilt. Sorrow. Anger. Fear.

Nasty beasts that tore at her competence, her professionalism.

The familiar tang of fear and rage settled like rot at the back of Quinn's throat.

Prior to his tours, that acrid combination had hit so infrequently he couldn't have named the emotions without examination. Now he knew them the second they descended. The only thing he didn't know was which person before him had summoned them this time—the best friend he'd found dangling by his neck, or the ex-wife who'd abandoned him.

He knew one thing: Anais didn't deserve the space in his head right now, even if she well deserved his rage. Ben was the one who mattered.

"Be still, man," he said, as Ben struggled beneath his hands, then looked at Anais. She could come back into his life as quickly as she'd left it, but that slapdash, incompetent disguise wouldn't fool anyone.

She stood still, staring at him as if she'd lost all her sense.

"Collar," he repeated to break through her shocked expression.

Don't think about her shock. It couldn't be anything more than fear that he'd yell at her—out her, maybe—but right now she only mattered inasmuch as she could help Ben.

He quickly smoothed his hands down his thighs, drying the suddenly sweaty palms, and then fixing them around Ben's head to keep him from moving it as she finally broke into motion out of the room.

Discipline had been drilled into him after the King had ordered Quinn's divorce and enlistment. He'd learned to follow their orders and he'd taught his body to follow his own. Self-discipline would see him through this, no matter how wrong it had been to see Ben hanging there, no matter how wrong it was for him to finally see Anais again like this, no matter how wrong it was that she'd changed so much. Falsely brown hair, eyes, tanned skin... Wrong. All of it.

The resolve to speak evenly was all that let him banish his anger as he turned his attention to Ben—who obviously didn't know who she was. "What's the doctor's name?"

"Anna," Ben answered.

A brown name for a bizarrely brown makeover.

Grasping for the only way he knew how to face such a situation, he attempted some levity to try and take the bleakness out of his friend's eyes. "The good news is, your arms still work great. I'm fairly certain I'll have a black eye later."

"You should've left me be," Ben said, his voice a painful-sounding rasp that could only come from an injured throat.

"I don't think so," Quinn muttered and then looked at the door. "Rosalie would be doomed to treason if I had, after she'd murdered me slowly in retribution."

Where the hell had Anais gone to get the brace—across town?

"What are you even doing here, Doc?"

"You've been avoiding my calls worse than my ex-wife," he said just as Anais came back into the room, the sounds of tearing straps accompanying her ripping the collar open, and perfectly complementing the color draining from her face. She'd heard him. Good.

He focused back on Ben, and that anger instantly diminished. "I came to see you, idiot."

Quinn accepted the collar and fitted it around Ben's neck for stability. Only when it was in place did he help Ben into the wheelchair.

Having tasks to do helped. Not looking at Anais helped. If he looked at her, the way his heart thundered in his ears, he'd say or do the wrong thing. That was something about the military that had worked for him—he'd never had to worry about how to say something, just whether he should say it or not. Soldiers appreciated blunt honesty more than diplomats. Something his brother Philip would remember after Quinn's first royal function.

"You should've let me hang," Ben said again, the words sinking into the middle of Quinn's stomach.

He shook his head. "I came to see you before I met with the King, which should give you some idea of my priorities right now. You're the last person in this room I'd let hang."

She'd hear that too. And she'd hear this… "Maybe even the last person in the world, though I might have to make an exception for any of *GQ*'s cover models. Even May's, and you know how that ended."

Petty. But it felt good to be just a little bit mean. Not that it could be all *that* mean—she was the one who'd left. And it made Ben almost smile, even the slight quirk of his lips was better than the desolation he'd seen in his friend's eyes.

"You're going to have to suffer me checking you over."

She'd returned with a bag, wearing a white jacket over what he could only classify as workout clothes, the shoulder of the jacket embroidered with the lie that she claimed as her name. Dr. Anna Kincaid.

Kincaid. Family name. Just not her maiden name. Or *his* name.

From the bag, she produced a stethoscope and handed it to him without his asking, but not without her hand trembling.

Afraid? Maybe she trembled with sympathy or worry for her patient, if she could even feel those human emotions.

He snatched the device, fitted it in his ears, and went about his job. His former job. He wasn't a medic anymore; yesterday had been his last day as a soldier.

Concentrating on the fast but steady thudding he heard through the ear pieces took more willpower than he'd have thought he had to spare. The urge to throw Anais over his shoulder like a caveman and take her somewhere to make her give him answers was just as strong. Maybe stronger. He'd been waiting seven bloody years for answers, and he'd never gotten a satisfactory one. He'd wait until he'd helped his friend, because today his luck had changed. She was here; answers were a matter of time.

Breaths sounded ragged but normal, all things considered.

"Let's get out of here. I think we could use some fresh air."

"Qui— Prince… Captain? There is a protocol…" Anais said from behind him.

He turned and looked pointedly at her embroidered shoulder. "I'm sure there is. Send whoever will be coming out to the garden, Anna."

"Yes, sir." She didn't flinch, though he noticed she also didn't look him in the eye.

Grabbing the handles of Ben's chair, he maneuvered them both right out the door and down the hallway. He knew the way to the garden.

He'd loved a girl in those gardens. A girl who apparently no longer existed.

How the hell had she managed to sneak back into the country under a different name, and start practicing medicine at a government facility, of all things?

Once they wheeled out into the fresh air, Quinn angled them to a bench so he could sit and be on eye level with the person he'd actually come to see. The one who obviously needed to talk.

Parked in a patch of summer sunshine, he waited. It wasn't the time for pushing. It wasn't the time to tell Ben he should want to live, or to tell him anything about his own condition. He'd listen. And he'd talk about other things. Be a friend. Be present.

Call Ben's fiancée and family as soon as he left.

Leave this Anais nonsense to figure out later. It wasn't really important. There was nothing she could say to him to make any of what had gone on between them better.

I never loved you.

I stopped loving you.

You were never that important to me...

What could she really say to explain leaving?

The desire to know was just a natural reaction to seeing her again, a summoning of that anguish he'd moved past at least a few years ago.

It didn't really matter. She didn't matter anymore.

Three hours and at least a hundred self-reminders not to think about Anais later, Quinn found himself outside the shut door to Dr. Anna Kincaid's office.

Anna Kincaid. Anna. Kincaid. The name summoned bile

to his throat. Seven years might as well have been seven minutes for the crush of desperation that had him wanting to claw through the door to reach her.

He'd managed to shove her to the back of his mind—for part of the time—and been present for his best friend, but it wasn't good enough. He'd heard the sparse number of words Ben had been able to speak, but in the long silences she'd filled his head again and again. When the psychiatrist had found them he'd been allowed to stay, but he hadn't learned much more about what had driven the attempt. All he really knew was what his eyes could tell him, and the memory of the strangeness he'd felt when he'd lost comparatively insignificant pieces of his own body to service. Some days still, he was shocked when he looked down at his hand and saw that not only the fingers but his wedding ring were gone. Some days, he still expected to find her beside him in the morning when he woke.

What he should be doing right now was making calls and going to the palace—where they'd expected him a few hours ago. Instead, he stood at her shut door. He couldn't hear her inside, but he could feel her in there, like heat on his skin.

If he felt like admitting it to anyone else—he barely felt like admitting it to himself—he'd felt her at the old family castle the moment he'd stepped into the building. At the time, he'd put it down to memories haunting him more than something in the present. But, standing there, he didn't even have to touch the door to feel her on the other side. His mangled hand hovered over the knob, and it heated his palm like light…

His hand wavered; he had to pull back from the knob. His arm felt seconds from a cramp, riddled with tension.

He didn't know which was worse—not knowing still, or that he could be so daft to even think for a fleeting second that anything about her could still warm him. The heat was long-simmering rage and pain. Nothing light about it.

If anyone noticed him standing here, feeling the energy emanating from her door when any rational person would just go inside…the psychiatrist would want to spend some time alone with him next.

He opened the door and it slammed directly into something, halting his forward march.

She stumbled out from behind the door, looking disoriented, but her stagger gave him room to enter and he took advantage of it, shutting the door directly behind him.

"Why were you standing there?"

"I was thinking about locking the door," she said without preamble. Then, redirecting his question, "Why were you standing outside the door?"

"Anais, I've had a hell of a day. I paused because I wanted to make sure I had control of myself and didn't come right in here and shake you hard enough to knock the brown off of you. What the hell are you playing at with this drab makeover and the name-change? Are you in the country illegally?"

She flinched, then shrugged back from him across the distance of her tiny office. He'd struck another nerve. That shouldn't please him, but the pink that flashed in her artificially tanned cheeks and the way she smoothed her hair down felt almost like satisfaction. He had seven years of jabs in reserve and, by the look of things, it wasn't going to get boring anytime soon.

"Of course I'm not here illegally. I had my name changed. Legally. Then I changed my appearance. My mother is getting older—she's got diabetes and had a heart scare last summer, not that I should have to explain myself. This is my country too, and I shouldn't have to lose it forever because I married poorly when I was young and naïve."

A tic in his right eyelid flickered at her return volley.

Definitely different from the Anais he'd known.

"How…?"

"Your brother changed my name for me quietly." She rubbed her cheek and he knew where the door had clocked her, but she stayed standing there, close enough—only because of the wall behind her—that he could reach out and touch her if he wanted to.

He did want to, so he shoved his hands into the well-worn fatigues he preferred these days, comfortable clothing he'd soon lose as he picked up a new mantle of duty.

"I went with Anna because it's close enough to Anais for me to still save myself if I start to say my old name. Kincaid is my grandmother's maiden name, so I have some attachment to it. Doctor, however, is legitimately mine."

Softness had always abounded in Anais. Tender heart. Soft, free-flowing wavy strawberry-blonde hair. Curves that bewitched him. Gentle aqua eyes. Youthfully plump cheeks and lips… Soft.

A red mark darkened that formerly plump cheek, outside the blush that had already faded. She'd had her ear to the door listening when he'd slammed it open. Not locking it. Or maybe not locking it yet, whatever she'd claimed.

She made herself sound even harder than she appeared. That physical angularity was by far the biggest change, and the one that had momentarily thrown him when she'd come into Ben's quarters. Not her hair color, her eye color, the glasses, or that suspicious tan… It was how square her jaw seemed now, the gauntness of her cheeks, and the now slender but apparently strong body supporting it all. Anna Kincaid was hard.

He didn't know what else to say.

For seven years, he'd had a million questions for her— mostly in the first couple of years when everything was hardest. But now, standing here, he didn't want to ask her why she'd gone. Those old wounds could pop back open

with the slightest prod. His chest already ached just looking at this shadow of his brightly colored Anais.

"Are you living back in Easton?"

"No. Are you still at the penthouse?"

"Yes," he answered. Why it had been so important to
him to come find her after speaking with Ben? "Is there
something you want to say to me?"

Like *I'm sorry*?

She shook her head, then seemed to change her mind
as the shaking turned into a nod, her voice going quieter.
"How do you know Lieutenant Nettle?"

"Served together. First tour," Quinn answered again.
Did she feel anything for him anymore? Besides anger?
Somehow, *he'd* earned *her* anger? Her anger, and the fact
that she wanted him gone was all he could make out. Her
eyes used to sparkle when she saw him, even the last time
she'd seen him—which she'd no doubt known would be
the last time—they'd still sparkled. But with them hidden under those unremarkable brown contacts, he couldn't
see it. Or it wasn't there. A wife who had feelings for her
husband…her ex-husband even…wouldn't look so hard
when he'd never wronged her. Never done anything wrong
but love her. Even a friend would look kindly upon a soldier returning home after seven years in a war zone, but
she just wanted him gone.

Over the course of his tours, he'd learned to fight his way
out of dodgy situations. Fight and survive first, complete
the mission second. He couldn't fight his way out of this.
He didn't even know where to start.

He could make her feel anger, maybe some polite curi-
osity, but nothing else. Touching her would just hurt him;
there was no Braille hidden on her flesh that would tell him
the truth, or what he wanted to hear: that she regretted leaving, that she'd suffered because of it, that she was sorry.

He forced his arms to relax, then thought better of it and

wrenched his mangled left hand from his pocket to present to her.

"Ben was there to help when my fingers were shot off." Seeing her blanch only emboldened him. With as much detail as he could summon from that day, he described the way the wedding band he'd still worn had become platinum shrapnel Ben had to pull from the remains of his palm. The way Ben had to cut away his dangling finger. "And that still hurt less than you."

Her eyes went round, with his hand held up for her inspection, and her breathing increased in speed and force; soon the heated air fanned his hand across the distance. The two fingers, thumb, and partial palm felt the flutter like the barest breeze.

"Get used to seeing me around here. I'll try to keep the cameras away, for Ben's sake."

Her open-mouthed breathing turned to choking, and he realized she was going to be sick a half-second before she turned and flung herself over her office trash bin and retched. Her whole body convulsed with the force of each spasm.

His stomach lurched too.

Damn.

They'd both changed. The last vestiges of the man who'd married her, who'd loved her, felt sick too, wanted to look away.

But the realist he'd had to become couldn't feel too badly. What had even made her sick? Hearing how he'd lost his fingers, or the idea the cameras that invariably ended up following him might catch sight of her?

As if it mattered. He should leave her there, let her get on with it, savor the little thrill of revenge that had run through him at her visceral reaction.

He wouldn't pull her hair aside and soothe her back. He wouldn't apologize for not softening the brutality of that situation for her, the way he'd softened it for his family.

She wasn't his family anymore. She'd been the one to leave. And he'd never gotten to say anything to her about it, since his family had shipped him off to boot camp directly afterward.

What was a little vomiting in that context?

CHAPTER TWO

NEVER BEFORE IN his homeland had Quinn felt so tense while riding in the back of a car. Every prior leave, he'd been able to disconnect that hyper-alert state traveling in a Humvee usually triggered while on duty.

First Ben, then Anais—both wrecked him. But going home for real—not just another leave—was the cherry on top of a terrible day.

Despite his late arrival—and he hadn't missed the fact that it had grown dark—Quinn had been requested to arrive by the main entrance. Usually he'd have gone around to a smaller, more private entrance.

It was showtime for the press.

But it looked relatively empty now, only a few cameras lingering to the side.

If he had to climb the grand entrance to go inside, he'd let himself out of the car. Quinn jumped from the back as soon as it stopped, thanking the driver over the seats, closed the door and jogged up, waving in passing at the few tenacious photographers who'd waited. No talking. No posing. He barely smiled.

Once inside, he bypassed servants, ignoring the familiar opulence he'd been raised in, and hurried across the foyer to the King's wing. Within two minutes, he knocked and opened the door to the King's study, but found Philip sitting behind the desk.

"You're not the King," Quinn murmured, making sure to gently close that door too.

His youthful habit had always been to bound through doors and expect them to close behind him—the same tactic he'd used with nearly everything: bound through, expect it to get sorted out in his wake. A tactic his family had spent years trying to talk him out of, and which his divorce and sudden soldier status had actually accomplished. Now he paid attention to doors. It was something small he could always control, and doors often presented a hazard or added protection. Doors now mattered.

Philip rose, checking his watch, but smiling anyway. "And you're not here at noon."

"No, I'm not." He should try to be amiable, but at that precise moment all he could hear was Anais's confession that Philip had changed her name. "Why didn't you tell me Anais was back in the country?"

He tried to sound calm, but even a dead man would've heard the bitterness in his voice.

Philip had rounded the desk, hand out to shake Quinn's, but he dropped it to his side with the question. "I was going to tell you when you got here. It seemed like an in-person kind of conversation to have. You've seen her already?"

"She's working at Almsford Castle with amputees. I went there to visit my friend, Ben Nettle; I told you about him. And that's…a story I really would rather not get into right now. But you know she's not fooling anyone by dipping herself in brown dye."

"She fooled me." Philip shrugged, and then reached out to grab Quinn by the back of the neck and pull him into a hug.

"That's because you're an idiot." It didn't feel like a time for hugging to Quinn, but he went along with it. A little brotherly ribbing was as playful as he could get right now. Clapping one another on the back a few times, they both retreated and Quinn went to help himself to a Scotch.

"She's changed more than that. I was surprised when she told me where she was going to work. I don't think she realized that the new facility was at Almsford Castle," Philip said, returning to his seat. "How was it to see her?"

Quinn eyeballed three fingers of booze since he had two fingers on that hand to measure with, and took it to the front of the desk to sit. "I don't know. Unpleasant. I guess. I don't want to talk about Anais."

"You brought her up."

"I did. Now I'm bringing up Grandfather. Is he here or did he go off on vacation for his rest?"

"He's here." Philip sat up straighter suddenly, his voice growing suspiciously softer.

The hairs on the back of Quinn's neck rose. This apprehension was more than he'd felt when deciding he needed to start serving the family and the people again as a prince. Something was wrong. "Where is he?"

"Sleeping. He spends most of the time sleeping now."

Those words had never fit their grandfather. Despite his advancing age, he was a vibrant man, always on the move. But the sober tones in which Philip delivered the news gave them weight, gave them truth. And gave him that feeling in the pit of his stomach for the third time that day.

The heat returned and he knew it for what it was: *helpless anger.*

"Was that something else you wanted to tell me in person?" He truly hadn't come home to fight with anyone, but it seemed to be all he'd been doing since he'd stepped foot into Almsford Castle.

The grimace that crossed Philip's face confirmed his suspicions.

"He didn't want you worrying when you were away," Philip admitted, his voice trailing off.

Quinn noticed for the first time the three-day growth of beard his always immaculately groomed brother now wore.

"He has good days and bad days, but is usually awake for a few hours in the late morning, early afternoon."

When Quinn had been supposed to come earlier.

"What's wrong with him?"

"He's an old man, Quinn. Time catches up to everyone."

He felt his head shaking before words—demands—began pouring out. "How, specifically, has it caught up with him? Heart failure? Some kind of cancer? Stroke? What's wrong? What happened?"

"Kidney failure is the big one right now. There are other more minor diagnoses, but his kidneys are the biggest worry. He's on dialysis, but he's too old for a transplant, and his body isn't holding up well to dialysis."

Quinn took a deep pull on the drink, considered draining it, then carefully placed it upon the desk.

"What does that mean?" He'd had training as an EMT in the military—hence Ben calling him Doc—but he wasn't actually a doctor. He hadn't dealt with dialysis in combat situations, so he didn't know anything about it. If he'd never gone into the military, he would've been better equipped to understand, assuming he'd gotten into medical school as he'd—as they'd both—planned.

Another life. He'd enjoyed his life as a soldier; it was his life as a prince that was stressing him out.

"Some people live a lot of years on dialysis, but his body just isn't strong enough. He's had the access port moved twice now. Keeps getting infected and he's running out of places to put it or the will to let them try another location. He's already said he won't be having another one placed." Philip headed for the decanter and poured his own drink.

After their parents' unexpected deaths when they were children, Grandfather had stepped up to fill the father role—even when he was busy running the country. Quinn just didn't know how to process this information. One more thing. A third person to save.

Well, second. Ben and Grandfather. He wasn't trying

to save Anais, and what could he even save her from? Another bad spray tan?

"Not to put pressure on you, but I'm hoping that having you around will give him the urge to fight a little longer," Philip muttered. "Then I wonder if that's selfish of me, but I can't help it. It's not looking good. I'm glad you're home. We need you. I need you here."

"I want to see him," he said, redirecting his thoughts to what mattered at this precise moment. He could only deal with what was before him.

"He's sleeping."

"And I want to see him. I can sit quietly at his bedside, Philip. I will be here tomorrow when he wakes, but I want to see him now. Let me prepare myself so I don't go in looking at him like he's a dying man when he sees me for the first time." He added, more quietly, "Let my first shock be when he can't see it. I've already had two shocks since I got home. I don't think I can look a third person I love in the eye like that."

A third person he loved. God help him, he'd done it again.

"Loved. Someone I loved. You know what I mean."

"Who was the second?"

Not Anais.

"Ben. I should feel bad that I didn't come here first and see Grandfather, but if I had Ben would be dead. He tried to hang himself in his room this afternoon, and I got there in time to stop him, get help, get him cut down… Which is why I have to see Anais again tomorrow, because I need to go back for Ben."

And he needed to make those calls still. God, this day really sucked.

His brother nodded to the nearly empty second tumbler. "Drink the rest first. Sounds like you're going to need it. Will you be staying here tonight?"

"No," he said first and then, after finishing his drink,

shrugged. "I don't know. Should I? I was going to go to my flat. Unless you think I should stay to see when he wakes?"

Philip shook his head. "You don't need to stay, but you look rough, Quinn. Your room is prepared if you want to stay. Might do you good."

Sleep would do him good. He stood again, but it took all the strength in him to follow his brother down the hallways to the King's suite.

Before they'd even entered, he heard the soft hums and beeps of life-saving equipment and knew Philip had been trying to soften the blow.

But Quinn smelled death. He knew the scent of it by now.

Anais stood at her favorite treadmill—the one she hadn't been on since Quinn's terrible cry for help had shattered her will to hide and sent her running toward him for the first time in years.

Her work day had ended over an hour ago, and Quinn was still on site, still with Benjamin Nettle as far as she knew—as far as everyone knew. A prince couldn't spend hours a day for three days straight in the building without word getting around.

What she didn't want to get around? That she'd been waiting for him today. Was still waiting for him. That knowledge would trigger too many questions and the conclusions she needed no one to reach if she wanted to stay. And she had to stay. Her departure from Corrachlean had meant leaving Mom, and they'd spent seven years apart. Visits had been impossible before Anna Kincaid had been born.

Quinn hated her Anna look—she could tell by the way he'd looked at her, as if she'd sprouted some horrifying, self-induced deformity. But she liked it in a way. It made her feel invisible. After fitting in—which she'd never truly done anywhere—being invisible was the next best thing.

But he hated more than her new look. He hated *her*.

And, really, what could she expect? Aside from expecting to not see him for a long, long time—or ever, if she'd had her way.

The treadmill whirred beneath her feet, and she took one of the safety bars to steady herself as she inched up the speed and the incline. Maybe exercise could wipe her mind, help her zone out and forget she was waiting for him.

The only way she'd kept going after they'd fallen apart was to practice willful amnesia. Not letting herself wonder about him or how he was doing, never thinking about how he felt or if he ever thought of her. She couldn't do that and keep going. Which probably made her the second person who hadn't been thinking about how Quinn felt—he never dwelt on anything that hurt. Not for himself. Not for her. Not for anyone, at least when they'd been married. She'd spent darned near a year trying to work him out, and all she had was: he liked sex with her and hated responsibility.

Then, two days ago, she'd learned something else—something that took her breath every time it replayed in her head, hundreds of times per day: losing his fingers hurt him less than she had.

Was he still suffering in the way she never let herself wonder if he was suffering?

She didn't want to believe it was true. His hatred was real, and he'd definitely wanted to hurt her, so it would be better if she could stop lingering over it. No matter what, her leaving had been kinder to both of them in the long run. If she'd stayed with Quinn until Wayne had followed through with his threats, Corrachlean's people wouldn't have been the only ones to think terribly of her; Quinn's opinion would've plummeted into earth too. At least he hated her now for something that was ultimately kinder. Even if she never wanted him to know that.

Maybe that was why, despite knowing he'd been at the facility the past two days, she hadn't been able to drag herself to Ben's room to ask him to speak with her. Or maybe it was something more cowardly. Maybe she was afraid that Ben would know who she was now, and she couldn't blame Quinn if he'd told him. He'd never promised to keep her secrets, and what loyalty did he owe her? Sharing something that was going on in your own life could be a kind of currency to get your friends to talk when they needed to.

"You're leaving notes for me now?" Quinn's voice cut across the cavernous ballroom-gymnasium, jolting her from her thoughts so that she had to grab the safety bars again to steady herself.

Would his voice always jolt her?

Heart hammering, she shut off the machine. At least she had the exercise to blame for the way her words came out, breathy and with effort. "I waited for an hour in the foyer, long past the time it started to look weird that I waited for you. Then I decided to write a note. The envelope was sealed, the front was as formal as could be."

Grabbing a towel, she dried herself off as she walked to meet him, pretending her legs wobbled because of the running too.

"I noticed." Quinn thrust the envelope back at her, and looked around the ballroom to make certain they were alone. The last thing he needed this week was to have to explain why he was ogling the doctor or being overly familiar. "And I'm here. What do you want?"

The nod to revenge he'd felt on leaving her there bent over the trash bin hadn't even lasted until he'd gotten out the door—and that hadn't even been a version of Anais who looked like his wife. While her hair and eyes remained the wrong color, her glasses were now gone and the hair pulled back from her face let him almost see her. Almost.

Her hand shook a touch when she took the envelope, and he swallowed the urge to lash out at her again, to shock her with some other brutality from the frontline—he had a thousand such story grenades to hurl.

"I just want to talk to you about something. Will you come to my office?"

"Why not here?"

"It's private."

Their last conversation had been on repeat in his head since it had ended. While he'd met with his brother. While he'd found out the new family secret: the King was dying. Even sitting by his grandfather's bed, he'd had her on repeat, enough to riddle out what had set her off.

She'd paled before he'd even mentioned the cameras. She'd been sick about him, not about herself. She still felt something, no matter what she pretended.

It would've been so easy to tell her to go to hell, ignore her, as he'd been more or less doing since that first day. To come when she was at lunch, leave when she'd gone home, and continue driving Ben up the wall by refusing to leave him alone in his misery.

But she wanted to talk. And, God help him, he still wanted to talk to her. Maybe this was his opening. Apologies started with regret and, whether she'd admit it or not, he could see she had regrets.

Quinn waved a hand for her to lead the way, and the relief on her face notched his hope higher. He had to pick up his usual leisurely pace to keep up with her and, directly in her wake, her scent channeled to him.

Sweaty, but she still smelled fantastic. Clean, but sweet. Sexy.

Her long, heavy locks had been pulled up high on her head, and the straightening she'd inflicted on it had come undone in the dampness. Waves stretched up from the bottom, where the mass had brushed against her bare back, gathering sweat. A shiver racked his body, raising chills all over him, and Quinn had to thank fate he was walking behind her rather than in her line of sight.

Getting wrapped up in hormones wasn't the right tack for this conversation—whatever it was going to be about.

Before she'd left him, he could've easily made any private conversation with her about what his body wanted.

He pulled his gaze to her feet, which seemed safest. Only feet attached to slender ankles, and then his eyes tracked up over the soft skin covering the newly acquired definition in her calves. Her thighs. Her rear…

The shorts she wore clung in a fantastically distracting manner and, just below, he could see the dark little mole that always wanted to be kissed, peeking and retreating from the hem of her shorts on the right as her clothing moved with each step.

By the time they reached her office he had to keep reminding himself of the objective, but every reminder was a little quieter than the hunger for her that had him shaking.

"It's hot in here," he muttered, dragging his jacket off and tossing it onto the back of one of the guest chairs.

"It gets warmer in here at night. Sorry. Would you like something to drink first?"

"I'm fine." He dragged the chair back and sat down, nodding for her to do the same. Hopefully outside of his reach. "But take out the contacts first."

"What?" She stilled, her expression shifting to something uncomfortably close to fear. "Why?"

As if she had anything to fear from him. Aside from something he might say to upset her…

"You want to talk to me? Great. I don't want to talk to Anna. I want to talk to Anais. When you've got them in, it's like I can't see you, but you can still see me. You want me to stay? Take them out."

"Anna wants to talk to you."

Anna. Right. This wasn't about them. This was about work.

Grabbing his jacket again, he rose and headed toward the door. Only a romantic idiot would've gotten his hopes up. It angered him that he'd gotten them up without even realizing it. She'd been gone for seven years, now she suddenly wanted to reconnect? Sure. *Dumbass.*

He'd reached the knob before she cracked. "Wait."

The sound of rustling came from behind him: drawers opening, things being dropped on the desk top. When he looked back, she had a contacts case and some fluid on the desk. Half a minute later, she had the contacts out and a tissue blotting her eyes.

"Still not used to them?"

"They're fine." She dropped the tissue on the desk, squared her shoulders, and came back around to sit as he'd done, chair turned, facing him. When she finally looked at him, his chest squeezed. Blue-green, like the southern seas on sunny white sand. Even with all the other changes, she was truly his wife in that moment. His eyes burned at the thought and he let his head bow forward until the burning passed, needing to get on with things, to keep from reaching for her, his tropical songbird masquerading as a pigeon.

And with the door closed, he couldn't smell anything but her.

God, this was a mistake.

"What did you want?"

Don't touch her.

Don't touch her. Don't touch her.

"I wanted to talk to you about Lieutenant Nettle."

Ben. Right. Good. He'd spent all that time at the facility for Ben, and she was one of his doctors. Made sense, if someone had a functioning brain.

Rather than saying anything else, he nodded. The sooner he let her get on with it, the sooner he could leave.

"I think it's been really great for him to have you here. I'm glad you keep coming back. Not just because you averted disaster; he wouldn't see anyone but staff otherwise. But now he's talking a little, mostly to you, I think. But he's having you stick around when the therapist comes, right?"

"Right," he said, then added, "What does Ben need? Just spit it out."

She shifted, tried to sit up straighter, but her shoulders already nearly reached her ears because of her stiff posture.

"It's not my place to say this—it has nothing to do with his limbs. I treat bone injury, not…soft tissue. But, since he's allowed you to become part of his care, I'm taking the liberty on the chance that you can help him."

Anais waited for his nod of understanding, and swallowed past the lump of fear in her throat. Since her mad scramble out of the country, she'd made a point of being good at eye contact. When you looked someone in the eye it established a connection that usually helped you in some fashion—intimidating muggers, letting professors know you meant business, letting patients know you were there and cared about what happened to them. Helpful.

Looking Quinn in the eye, she felt small. And hideous. The contacts didn't change her vision in any way, but they made her feel hidden, and unseen was safe. Now she had to dig deep for the courage she hadn't even glimpsed since she'd seen him.

One piece chipped free from her Anna armor, and she was stuttering with tears burning.

"He's got more damage than just his legs." Her voice was too high, too shaky.

Quinn's stormy eyes lifted to hers again, narrowed. "I haven't seen his chart and getting him to talk about his injuries is almost impossible. Was he shot? I know about the IED. They throw off shrapnel."

"He wasn't shot. There were a few abdominal wounds from shrapnel, but most have healed nicely." She should've rehearsed this. The words didn't even want to move through her throat. "He lost one testicle."

Anna would be stronger. She'd look him in the eye again. It took force, and strength she didn't really have at the time, but she met his gaze. The description of damage took the disappointment out of his eyes; he'd focused on Ben, just as she'd hoped.

"They were able to restore urinary function. But there's more…" She saw understanding dawn on his face and, the second it came, she wished she hadn't needed to tell him.

CHAPTER THREE

"MORE TO RESTORE?" Quinn's words came slow and low, as if tension and gravity made him pause for a breath after each word.

"Repairing areas with vascular damage." She clarified, "They did what they could the first time, but it didn't heal properly. The surgeon is confident he can restore full function, but Nettle—Ben—won't talk to anyone about it. I even tried once, early on, because the staff GP said he'd gotten nowhere either. The psychiatrist also had no luck. He shut me down really quickly."

Quinn took it in dead silence.

Was he getting it? She couldn't tell if it was his usual tactic—letting the bad wash over him like water off a duck's back—or if he was processing. There was concern on his face, but his silence didn't give any hint to his thoughts. She'd have to put it to him straight.

"I think if you talk to him about the procedure and why he should have it, he might listen…"

He reached behind him and rubbed the back of his neck, finally pulling his gaze away from her for a moment. "He's talking a little, but I don't want to push him. It's a delicate balance, right now."

Like Quinn was talking a little. It was only an opening, but one she'd never got before. Talking about problems, at least his friend's problems, might be within his capabilities. He hadn't said no. He just needed convincing.

Anais stood and dragged her chair closer to him, close enough that their knees almost touched.

"He's got a chance at a normal life if he has the procedure. I doubt he feels like getting married knowing he won't be able to father children, or…be…with his wife." Don't linger on the sex, even if she knew Quinn would definitely get that rationale. "I think that particular injury is an even bigger one mentally to him than his legs. It's the reason for how you found him, I'm sure of it."

Quinn's expression hadn't changed—concerned, maybe a little out of his depth and horrified at the idea of talking to his friend about something so personal. But what got more personal than asking your friend to cut your dangling fingers off?

She kept going. "With the surgery, he could have a normal life. We can work with him on his mobility— his life won't ever be entirely normal because he's a double amputee, but he could have a family."

A family. Something she'd wanted with Quinn. Something she still wanted, but had never been able to picture with anyone else. The word had become like a weapon, a word that could hurt them both. But if she couldn't reach Nettle, she had to reach the person who could.

Whatever it took.

Before she could think too much about it, she took his left hand, forcing him to look at her again.

"What are you doing?" he asked, his stormy gray eyes sliding from their hands to her eyes, but lingering heavily over her mouth.

He started to pull away.

"Wait!" She transferred his hand to lie on her palm and traced the jagged edge left after the blast. "If you could have back these parts that were taken from you, if you could have them, fully functional, wouldn't you want it? I know this was terrible for you, and I haven't—" she swallowed "—I can't close my eyes without seeing it."

Her throat squeezed so hard she could barely breathe, let alone talk. Blessedly. Those weren't the words she'd needed to say. This wasn't about her. It was about him. About Ben.

"Imagine you could have a place for your wedding ring, the next time you married." She felt tears slip as she said the words. "Wouldn't you want that? I know…it didn't… go the way…either of us hoped it would, but sometimes…"

"I have no desire to get married again." The words dropped like lead.

A sharp jerk pulled his hand from hers and she lifted her eyes to his, not even trying to hide the tears quivering in her vision.

She'd messed it up, yet more proof they never knew how to talk to one another. This wasn't supposed to be about them. How had it become about them?

Pressure on her neck made her lift her head, and the next instant his mouth covered hers. The moment stretched out and she measured it in breaths and heartbeats. One breath she was in her chair, the next she was in his lap, her sluggish mind struggling to catch up.

All she knew in that moment was an ache that seared into her. His mouth, hot and desperate, on hers echoed the frenzied need crouching in her own breast since the moment she'd heard his laugh. She was a silly, naïve twenty-year-old again, starved for his kisses, for his touch, for the heat of him against her.

When she opened her eyes, it hurt to see him. His brows were wrenched, as if touching her hurt more than helped. As if he tortured himself with every kiss, but couldn't stop.

She didn't want to stop. She didn't want to feel him shaking or the mingling of pleasure and bitter need that twisted her insides. But she couldn't stop.

Her arms came around his shoulders, pulling him close, reveling in his solidity, the breadth of him. His face had matured; his body had as well. He was a new man, but still the same.

His arms around her waist bent her toward the floor, and he paused only long enough to shove chairs violently away, making a space for them.

There was no way for reason to intervene, not when his unfamiliar and heady mass pressed her into the cold wood floor, and his hands began frantically pulling at the material separating them.

Her tank top came up and her front-clasp bra popped open at his insistence. He only took his mouth from hers to turn his attention to her breasts.

Her breath left her and she moaned so loudly that he lunged back over her, covering her mouth again with his own, absorbing every tortured gasp he ripped from her.

Before she registered movement, he'd stripped her from the waist down. She could only hold his mouth to hers, needing his kisses to continue blocking out the world. Needing to fill her lungs with him.

Tenacious, unhesitating, he pulled her legs around his hips, and launched himself into her.

Dizzy and breathless, only his mouth kept the broken sobs of her regret and need from echoing through the whole facility.

Like a wild thing, he set a thundering pace, hollowing her out and tearing down those carefully constructed walls of protection. Anna was gone. Anais was too. All thoughts gone. Nothing left but this need to get closer, to wrap her legs around him and pretend that the years in between never happened. Forget the bad times. Forget the end. Even forget the wedding. Pretend she didn't know it was only lust and anger driving him. This was hate sex for him. That horrible need to be closer. They might never be cured of it but it had been twisted by her leaving, and by his never showing up to begin with.

Still, she hung in that heartbeat where she'd still believed they could have that future she'd so desperately wanted. With this man—the only man who could bullhead through her reservations and convince her to act against her best interests.

He was with her, connected, inside her, but leaned away until it was his idea to return for another desperate, suffocating kiss. That frequent distance kept her from reaching for him until he deigned to return to her.

The last time she'd held him, he'd still been a boy. A decidedly handsome, sexy boy, but now, broad-shouldered and deliciously heavier than he'd been, he still felt like hers. Angry, but hers. Wanting to punish her, but still part of her.

It was wrong. All of it. The sex. Wanting to see him. Wanting to know him… Wrong. Stupid and wrong.

Stretched too taut, the thread of her pleasure snapped, and the first wave of her climax blasted through her, but she was too far gone for moans or any sound. It was all she could do to keep breathing.

When he stiffened and jerked, his broken breaths told her he'd come with her, and there had been no barriers in those few moments. Not even the sort that would prevent pregnancy.

Pretend it was still then. Back when they'd had a future. When she'd have felt only bliss at the idea of having his child. Before she'd learned how much to value a quiet life.

Quinn relaxed against her, his stubble-roughened cheek to her shoulder, rapid breath fanning her hair.

What were they doing? Why had she kissed him back?

Her hands ached to smooth over his back, to relearn the body she'd once known. To comb through his hair, trace his jaw and feel the rasp of his whiskers against her fingertips. She wanted to luxuriate in the tactile experience his body could bring. Just hold on and pretend for a little longer.

Instead, she curled her fingers to her palms to keep from stroking his skin. As soon as she got control of her thoughts, of her mouth—as soon as she could stand the idea of him looking at her again—she'd push him away. Off her, out of her...

No words came from her, not out loud, but it was as if he heard her anyway. Quinn lifted himself, off and away from her, severing their connection before he'd even gotten control of his heart.

On his knees between her legs, still mostly dressed, he rested and silently looked over her naked body. A heated look, at least. He still wanted her. This could be the first in a long, tangled back and forth—something she wouldn't be strong enough to withstand. Or it could be another sign that it was once again time to run.

She pulled her tank top down to cover her breasts, and scooted back to sit up, legs together. As if that would make her less bare to him.

What could be more heady than knowing how little effort it had taken to have her? A kiss. Just one kiss. And she'd practically begged him.

"I need my shorts." She didn't want to crawl past him to reach them, but she would if she had to.

Without a word, he shoved the crumpled garment at her, and climbed to his feet, righting himself. Tucking in. Zipping up.

"If you're wondering, that was goodbye," he announced as he bent to look under the desk for his shoe. "That's all."

The goodbye she'd denied him.

"Right," she managed, no words coming to mind that would provide her with the same emotional distance. He'd just announced the end of whatever they'd had, as if it hadn't ended once already. That was what he'd been doing—ending things?

He'd had a goal, but why had she gone along with it? Because...chemistry.

Because she was still vulnerable to chemistry. Because in some ways she'd be forever stupid.

It had blinded her before. Blinded him too. They'd tried

to build a marriage on chemistry—the height of bad reasons to get married.

If he'd loved her, if he'd ever felt anything for her besides lust, he would've listened when she'd tried to tell him about the photos, her blackmailer. He would've helped her. Helped them. He would've cared what was happening to her. But he hadn't. Everything always just magically worked out in Quinn Land. Fate was kinder to him than it had ever been to her, and he took it for granted.

One last anger-filled time was his version of goodbye. There weren't feelings attached. For either of them. She had regret, and chemistry, and that was plenty. How much worse would it be to still love him and have him never able to feel the same?

Even weakness and chemistry-fueled unprotected sex on her office floor was better than that.

Snagging the shoe, he straightened his sock and crammed the shoe back on.

Following his lead, she shimmied into her underthings and stood.

"Are you going to talk to Nettle?" There. Those were words. The thing she'd actually wanted to talk to him about before all this insanity happened.

"I'll talk to him."

She turned to grab her shoe and heard the door close.

Whatever. She sat down and put the shoe on.

Showering, changing, and going home would help. Get the scent of him off her. Clothe her far too bare form. Drink tea while not letting on to Mom that anything was wrong. And sleep…

Leaning over the desk to get her bag, she noticed the large envelope she'd prepared for this talk.

He'd left without the literature. *Of course he had.*

Snatching the envelope from her desk, she ran out after him.

Just before he got to his car, she made her way through

the door at the front of the building. "Quinn... Prince Quinton."

Get it together.

He turned and looked at her, left the car door standing open and met her halfway. "What else?"

"You forgot this." She pushed the envelope into his hand—the lights in front of the building harsh against the falling darkness.

No contacts. No freaking real clothes. Hair back. Proof yet again that fate refused to do her any favors.

Except one thing: no one was really about to notice her eye color, or how closely she resembled the former Princess. No one outside his employ, at least. Five cars parked in front of and behind his. How much security did he need to come to a rehabilitation center for soldiers?

"It's literature on the procedure. How it's done. Case studies. So you can prepare your talk."

With Nettle. It was on the tip of her tongue to call the soldier by his last name again—it was a distance tactic she'd been relying on, and had noticed it bothered Quinn—but she couldn't take a single drop more drama and hostility between them. Not until she had time to think. Until she had time to prepare for the possibility that she could've just irresponsibly conceived with her ex.

Once his hand closed on the envelope, she spun and headed back inside. Shower. Shower first stop. Then get the hell out of there.

When Quinn had agreed to come home, he'd thought it would go a little differently.

Summer had arrived, so naturally he'd assumed there would be loads of parties to attend where he would meet women. Drinks. Philip would fill his schedule with meetings, dinners, and appearances, telling him what to do, when, where, and what was expected of him. All that.

All he had so far was news of his grandfather's terminal

illness, a friend who'd tried to kill himself, an ex-wife he couldn't keep his mind or his damned hands off, and now a tricky emotional situation he was utterly unequipped to deal with.

And a distinct lack of drinks.

Slamming the door to his penthouse, Quinn tossed the envelope Anais has shoved at him onto the counter, and made a beeline for the fridge.

He grabbed a tumbler, threw some ice into it, and turned toward the liquor cabinet, only to stop. That route out of his kitchen had been blocked by large lidded plastic crates. Stuff he was supposed to deal with too. Seven years' worth of junk that people had just been sticking into crates for him...and he'd been ignoring for every leave.

But it was better duty than that penis conversation.

He backtracked and went the other way around the kitchen to reach for the rum, which would at least get the taste of her out of his mouth.

Instead of kissing her, he should've asked how to start this conversation.

He drained the glass entirely, felt his stomach lurch, and put the glass back down.

The man knew what parts were malfunctioning. It was his body. They'd told him that he could probably get it fixed. He knew these things already.

How would Philip handle this task?

Something heartfelt. Make an appeal to his better nature—whatever that would amount to.

He poured himself another glass and took another pull on the rum, and put the tumbler down.

Anais had never approved of drinking, for any reason. No wine with dinner. No beer after an arduous exam. Strip poker was fine, but not with shots. Not for her. And when she'd gone he'd thrown himself into spirits whenever the opportunity presented itself. Boot camp and deployment had probably saved him from becoming an alcoholic that first year.

He should watch the drinking since she'd strayed back into his life.

He turned his attention to the first crate, lifting the lid and riffling through its contents.

At the bottom of the stack of papers requiring his attention was a large yellow envelope, crammed with documents.

He flipped it over and read: *Divorce of Prince Quinton Corlow and Princess Anais Corlow née Hayes.*

Right. Bloody timely. He flung the packet over his shoulder in the vague direction of the sofa, and went back to the crate.

Gifts.

Books.

Things to be looked at later, when he'd not drunk enough rum to make his eyes go blurry.

A photo album filled with pictures taken during their whirlwind marriage.

Half a crate's worth of quasi-attentive sorting painful garbage was enough for one night. There really wasn't enough rum in his place for further torture.

Flopping one leg over the edge of the crate, he pushed the remaining material to the far end to make room for what he had to put back in.

A white-handled gift bag tumbled out of the moving pile of stuff, hit the bottom of the crate and spilled a small unopened package wrapped in pale blue paper and a silver bow onto the floor.

His heart stopped the moment he saw it.

It must've been the first crate the palace staff started packing for him. Copies of divorce papers. The gift he'd bought Anais for their first anniversary—the one they hadn't made it to—an engagement ring she'd never gotten before the wedding because they'd impetuously eloped.

He swallowed, then kicked the small box back to the

side. Stuffed into a crate by someone who didn't know its value. He put it right back there, suddenly too bitter to care about the small fortune buried under papers by his boot.

Enough of that.

He began dumping the bits he'd sorted out right back into the crate. Too much. All too much to deal with tonight, when all he really wanted was a shower and some sleep.

CHAPTER FOUR

STILL MARRIED.

The words rattled around in Quinn's head, as they'd been doing since he'd seen the morning news.

Sitting across from his ranting brother on the naughty schoolboy side of the King's desk at least made the news feel real, if still unpleasant. He'd never inspired his brother to rant before. Father, Mother, even Grandmother, God rest them. The King never ranted, though that sad, disapproving shake of his head always hit harder.

But, as he watched his brother pace and growl at him, he fully realized how things had changed.

Grandfather was dying. Philip now worried about these things, and felt as if he'd inherited a problem.

Quinn had always done his best to care when he was being lectured, but he never really had. Things always worked out, somehow.

Well, except for his marriage.

His day had started with a phone call and a number of emails, all directing him to programs and pages with the kind of annoying news reports they'd always lobbed at Anais, whether she deserved them or not.

They had always been big on inappropriate sex and full of tales of devious female conniving. And big on underestimating him—though they weren't wrong about him having wildly inappropriate...

Who was he kidding?

It was appropriate.

It felt appropriate.

It felt like a damn lightning bolt—illuminating to the point of scorching.

One enterprising journalist had caught a picture of them together and had gone off to investigate the court records of their divorce. Although apparently there were no court records. It must be a mix-up. It *had* to be a mix-up.

"Are you listening, Quinn?"

"Yeah, I hear you. You're angry. You don't know how it could have happened. I wish I had the answer for you."

Philip sat back down and stared hard at the photo of Quinn and Anais. "What's she wearing?"

"Workout clothes. She…runs. Or maybe boxes. I don't know. She works at the rehabilitation facility. She probably exercises all the time. It wasn't some kind of cheap ploy to get my attention."

Even though it had gotten his attention, or just focused his attention.

"When did you start defending her? You never…"

"You never attacked like this before. I know you're stressed out, but she literally did nothing wrong." Nothing that was caught on camera, he prayed. "She'd been working out when I left Ben for the evening, and since she wanted to talk to me about his care, I went to speak with her. The documents she's handing me in that photo are something to do with the medical care. I haven't read them yet."

"Great."

"Yeah. So calm down. I saw the envelope of official divorce documents last night when I was going through the big crates of rubbish accumulated for me since I enlisted. I'll go home, find the papers, and you can show them to the press. Then all this goes away." Those words should've been easier to say. Shouldn't be making his stomach churn.

"Except that she's here, and now the people *know* she's

here." Philip rubbed both hands over his face. "Her name change means nothing. It'll probably be used as evidence of more crimes they can attribute to her. I tried to warn her this could happen."

Because, no matter how horrified Philip had been by their inappropriate and spontaneous marriage, he'd always liked Anais. He still did, Quinn could see. This didn't only upset him because it was bad publicity, no matter how inopportune the timing.

"Doesn't matter. She can't win in this situation anyway, Philip. She was reviled as my wife, and then crucified when she left me. One or the other scenario should've made the people happy, but it didn't. This is just melodrama to sell papers."

"You always say that."

"It always goes away," Quinn tried again.

"No, someone always makes it go away. But I'm not doing that this time. You show the papers to the press. This is your first official royal duty: cleaning up your own mess. I have actual things to do that don't involve monitoring or refereeing your love life."

"How is this my mess? I was away in freaking boot camp when the divorce was arranged." Quinn couldn't help but complain a little; he was being blamed for not knowing exactly what a divorce by royal decree entailed? "I'll handle it. But I didn't leave her. I didn't ask to go into the military or to be divorced. I went where I was told, and did what I was told."

He'd never wanted to go into the military, but had ended up there because he couldn't think straight enough after she'd gone to make a counter offer, or even string together an argument. She'd gone, then it'd felt as if his family had given up on him too—shipped him off to be someone else's problem.

"You did," Philip said, anger dispelled with the quiet words. "And we're all proud of you for the sacrifices you made for your country, and the man you've become. But now that man can handle…"

"I said I'd take care of it." Quinn cut him off. Philip might be the heir to the eternal throne, but he wasn't wearing the crown yet. "Don't be too proud. I did what I had to do in the military—made a new family, found a way to fit and belong. Then I was told to come home and give that new family up, so I have. I'll sort this out, as you've ordered. My love life is fully off your plate."

Philip didn't argue further; he didn't look as if he knew quite what to think or say in that moment.

"Is he having a good day?" Quinn changed the subject as he rose and gestured to the door leading to the King's wing.

"He was doing well when I saw him before you arrived."

"Has he seen the papers?"

"Yes."

"Then I'll go and reassure him now."

As Quinn strode from the room, he heard Philip swearing under his breath behind him.

Upset a little? Seemed to be his habit, upsetting everyone. Including himself.

A good brother wouldn't have admitted feeling abandoned by his family in his hour of need. He'd have sucked it up and let them continue in blissful ignorance, just happy he'd turned his pathetic life around. But that was something he'd learned from the military: bluntness had its advantages.

A soft knock on the ornate carved door to his grandfather's bedchamber, and he opened it enough to peek inside.

Awake.

Sitting by the window in the sun, book in hand.

"Come." The once robust voice sounded brittle and diminished. Whatever reserve of righteous anger Quinn had built up likewise diminished.

"It's Quinn," he said then let himself in, paying mind to the gentle closing of the door. "I just wanted to reassure you that the situation with Anais will be sorted out."

"Oh? Well, that's good then. I'm sure you and Philip can handle it."

Yes. Philip could handle it, Grandfather would take comfort in that, so Quinn didn't correct him. "Don't worry yourself over it."

"She looks strange with her hair dark. Does it look better in person?" Grandfather gestured to a newspaper on the table beside him.

"Not particularly," Quinn admitted, grinning despite the subject as he moved another stately wingback closer to where the King sat. "She looks like she's playing dress-up in someone else's skin too."

"Left a mark on her too, I think."

Their divorce.

Quinn couldn't find words for that. He nodded, and turned as another knock came, followed by the sound of a trolley being pushed into the room. "Lunch or tea?"

"Lunch," the King's valet answered, stopping nearby and settling a tray across the King's lap to begin serving.

"I'm not hungry right now, Henry. Perhaps just tea."

Quinn gently dismissed Henry and headed to the cart to pour two cups, then peeked beneath the cover on the delivered plate and announced it cod, beans, cheese, good bread. The King didn't get excited about food like a soldier did. Or even a former soldier. Anything that looked this good? Definitely worth being excited over. Unless you were terribly ill.

"I could send for some soup, not so heavy?" Carefully, he transported the cups along with a small plate of cookies. Maybe he could tempt him there at least.

"Have I told you how much you remind me of your father, Quinton?"

"No. If you had, I would've said you were lying." It took effort to fake this upbeat air, but it would be less upsetting to both of them if he did. At least he could pretend things were normal, as he'd been doing with Ben, he realized. He'd been pretending with everyone but Anais, and just now, Philip. "I remember my father well, and Philip is the one who is like him."

"Later on. When he was a young man, he was like you. Bold. Carefree. Full of energy."

He wanted to talk, so Quinn would listen even if the words made no sense. And when his energy had depleted, Quinn would go home and read those damned papers and maybe call Ben, see what had been going on at the center today, as the press went into full-blown attack mode.

By the end of her workday, between watching the gathering throng of reporters forced to stay outside the Almsford gates, and the many worried calls from Mom to hear about the same at home, Anais had worked up a head filled with lightning.

They followed her from the castle to Quinn's penthouse, but knew enough to stop in the lobby while she stormed on through the shining white marble of her former home, past the familiar gray-haired guard at the reception desk, and straight for the elevator.

"Miss?"

When she pressed the button and the doors slid open, only then did she look back and saw the shock of recognition on his weathered face. "Haven't you heard, Alvin? Quinton and I are still married."

Before he could say anything else, she stepped inside and pressed the button for the top floor, sending the box rushing toward the heavens. Or, more probably, elevated Hell.

One of the world's fastest, finest elevators rocketed her straight to some kind of elevated perdition framed in gleaming marble and modern lines.

Contemporary in every way, the building had always driven home just how badly she fit there. She'd been a long-term visitor there, nothing more. It had never been her home any more than the place where she'd grown up had been. She hadn't missed it for a second when she'd gone, even when she'd missed Quinn so badly she could only go through the motions of everyday life—excelling where she was supposed to excel, but it had all been a way of getting her from her morning bed to her bed at night, and the blessed oblivion of sleep.

When she'd done her rotations in the psychiatric wards during medical school, she'd understood how people ended up addicted to drugs, or addicted to anything that took them out of their lives. She'd felt addicted to sleep, though came to realize it was depression muted to the world by an over-achieving personality.

Reaching Quinn's door, she pounded without stopping until, wild-eyed, he swung it open. "Please, do come add to my terrible day. If you're here to yell at me too, stow it. I don't know what's going on any more than you do."

"You didn't call your army of lawyers?"

"Not yet." He left her at the door and went back to digging in one of three massive crates taking up the largest part of the living room—at least the parts not covered by furniture or clutter. "I thought I'd start by digging up the divorce papers."

"And they're in those crates?"

"I saw a marked envelope in one of them the other night while self-medicating with rum," he practically sneered. "But these things are full of junk and I can't remember what I did with the packet."

He dove back in, snatched up a packet of something, examined it, then chucked it over his shoulder before diving back in.

"What did the papers say?" Since she was there, she'd darned well help. The sooner the papers were found, the sooner the press would lose interest in her. She tossed her bag onto the counter and dumped another onto the floor, then sat in the middle to start sorting. The one good thing about being super angry while being around him? There wasn't anything endearing about the man right now. Or sexy. All she felt was alternating waves of anger and terror, back and forth like a pendulum. None of that was sexy, which was the one part of it she could be thankful for.

"I didn't open it. Why on earth would anyone open divorce documents to read them? They weren't written by John Grisham." He copied her method and resumed sorting. "Wait, you're annoyingly organized. Where are your copies of the papers?"

Her copies! She could almost laugh, "That's adorable. You think I was included in things. No. I went to the States, and no one bothered to look up my address, I guess. I signed the papers before I left. I don't even know what happens after a royal divorce, but I signed the bloody papers."

"Yeah, I—" His pause bid her look at him again.

Uneasiness crept up her spine. "You what?"

"I don't really remember any of that." He looked genuinely confused—not a trace of sarcasm there, just befuddlement.

"You don't remember signing your divorce papers?"

He shook his head, brows pinched above eyes tracked to the side, as if searching his memory.

"Didn't that strike you as odd?"

That question earned her all his attention.

"Odd? What struck me as odd was that my wife had just left me. That I was suddenly enlisted in the military. That medical school was permanently off the table. Those things struck me as odd. Shocking and odd."

Anais had been biting her tongue since she'd arrived, mostly trying to be more civil than the crackling in her ears demanded, but this quintessential Quinn manner of conflict resolution had her working not to shout at him.

"You want to do this now?"

"No, I wanted to do this seven years ago. I'm through waiting."

She could tell by his tone that he had worked up a lung-ful. And she'd be damned if she cowered behind his rage.

"Fine. Now it is. But back then? If you'd been paying any attention, you would've seen it coming. I didn't leave you spontaneously. It happened over months. I needed your help—I needed more than your arrogant certainty that things would just work out, and you shut me down every time I reached out to you." Anais climbed to her feet. At least she could run if she needed to; sitting on the floor made her feel even more vulnerable than this conversation.

He snorted, "When did I shut you down?"

Before answering, and because she wanted to scream, Anais looked around the room for the envelope while taking deep, slow breaths.

"There was your answer for everything: sex. Or tell-ing me my concerns weren't important and that I should forget about them. *Don't worry, don't worry, don't worry. Everything will be fine.*" She flipped open the next crate, somehow doing all the talking. "Except that's not how life works. Things weren't fine. The people hated the idea that I was married to you, and every day it got worse. And guess what? They still hate it! I'm not allowed to go back to work until we get this sorted out, so help me find the papers. What color was the envelope?"

"Yellow. Large. Big black type on a white sticker. *Divorce of Prince Quinton Corlow and Princess Anais Corlow née Hayes.*" He answered that first, then looked back. "And why would you get fired? Anais Hayes doesn't even work at the clinic. Dr. Anna Kincaid works there. She might have a passing resemblance to Anais, but there's little else of Anais there."

"You're right. Anais died seven years ago." The words ripped out of her before she had a chance to consider them, hot on the edge of tears. She continued working through the things in the second crate, picking up every item only long enough to verify it wasn't a yellow envelope.

"You started this insane self-coloring program then? But Philip only changed your name this year."

She ignored the question, pushing back where she felt least exposed. "Please, let's talk about how, in order to come home, I had to engage the help of the Crown Prince to change my name without the public finding out. Having to rely on royal favors to live a life that those same royals wanted nowhere near them? Made my life *perfect*."

Quinn pushed a full crate out of the way. "Because it was so perfect after you left? Great. Good to know you didn't suffer for a second after going. I always wondered. You went to Shangri-La. I went to a war zone."

Another shot that sailed straight and struck her right in the *subgenual cingulate cortex*—aka Guiltville, Her Brain.

"Don't even pull that with me." She grabbed a stuffed animal and winged it at his head. "I didn't say that at all. And you didn't care the whole time we were married. I needed you and you didn't give a damn, so why would you care after I left? You wouldn't. You didn't. I will concede that you went somewhere awful afterward. I went to a shoddy walk-up in a shoddier neighborhood in the Rust Belt—which might as well have been a war zone."

"So, you felt right at home?"

Right where she belonged. She couldn't even argue with that, but he'd share his load of the blame.

"I guess. But, since we're on the subject, I know all this bluster was just you not wanting to admit that my leaving was not all me. It was you. And you don't want to talk to me about something that hurt and scared me. Still. It's easier to hurl blame." She gave up on the second crate and headed to the one he'd already searched, and turned it over again.

She needed this to be done before Wayne came back out of the woodwork with a barrel of shame and denigration in tow.

* * *

Quinn couldn't do this, not with her refusing to look at him. The papers could wait, but he was through waiting. He prowled over to her, took her elbow, and turned her to face him.

"I don't know what you're talking about. You mean I didn't want to spend all our time together fixating on the media? Yes. That's right. It did no good for anyone; it just made you more upset. That doesn't mean I didn't care. I cared. I cared about you more than anyone."

"I was looking for solutions!" She jerked away. "You remember those. That's what you're looking for with Ben. Who, by the way, I love that you're helping. Talking to him and seeing him through this. But it only goes to show how little you did that with me—to show that you were never mine, not really. We had chemistry. We had wild chemistry, and that was all you needed or wanted."

She spun away, her arms folding over her head in a cage, her fingers fisting in her own hair. The hopelessness of her action silenced him.

Her version of the downfall of their marriage didn't at all match his. Their problem was…well, he still didn't know, but it wasn't stupid rumors and paparazzi. Although anger that she couldn't see past that problem when it had become so present today wouldn't help him understand what had really happened back then.

What had she said? She'd needed him and she'd been scared.

The word sucked the anger out of him. "What were you scared of?"

"Does it suddenly matter?" She returned to the crate, back to sorting through the stuffed animals and cards, back to not cooperating. A few minutes ago she'd wanted to talk; now she didn't?

He needed a freaking compass to keep up.

"You said you were scared and that I was avoiding talking to you about it. So, what were you scared of?"

She pushed back from the last crate and gestured around the room, "Where were you when you last saw the envelope?"

Still not answering. Not looking at him. Not hearing him?

This whole conversation had been too heated, too angry, not something to inspire sharing of confidences. With a sigh, he dragged a chair over, gesturing for her to take it, and asked more gently, "What were you scared of?"

Anais sat in the chair and leaned forward, putting her elbows on her knees—the way he often sat when angry or stressed—and then systemically turned her head and scanned every inch of the room, still not answering him.

Something inside him didn't want to accept that she'd been scared. The word rankled.

He understood fear now, really understood it. He hadn't then; nothing in his life had ever been so bad that he couldn't face it before his first tour. But Anais had grown up differently than he had. She'd come from a poor urban area, she'd worked hard to get scholarships and the best grades she could, but her life before university—and anytime she'd gone home on holidays—was anything but safe and comforting. She'd been acquainted with real fear long before he had. And the idea that he'd left her alone with that fear curdled his stomach.

"Anais?" He said her name softly as he dropped into a crouch before her, eye-to-eye with her where she leaned in his favorite position. She bolted back, ramrod straight, wariness darkening her unnaturally brown eyes.

"Can we take out the contacts for good now? The cat is out of the bag, Princess. Brown contacts aren't going to hide you anymore."

Reflexively, she rubbed the base of her throat, then

twisted her hands in her lap. "I guess they weren't as effective as I'd hoped."

"Didn't work on me." He smiled, tired but willing to let go of his anger to get through to her.

It worked. She reached up and plucked the contacts from her eyes, and when she focused on him again those blue-green eyes warmed him like a hand reaching out from the past to pull him back to her. As if the past seven years had never happened. But then he remembered it had. And he remembered why he'd crouched before her.

"Thank you." He tried again, "What scared you? Please tell me."

"Something happened that I didn't want anyone to know about. It would've ruined…everything." She gestured helplessly, and looked back toward the kitchen. "I need to throw these away."

When she looked back at him, she squinted over his shoulder and leaned forward slightly, staring across the room. "I think it's under the sofa."

A secret. She'd tried to share a secret with him, to ask for his help, and he'd not listened to her? The idea was so unthinkable that when her digression came he was thankful to turn his attention to the sofa.

He'd thrown it. The memory swam back through the rum-soaked haze that had separated him from it, and he rose to go fetch the documents.

A moment later he had the envelope. Anais joined him, sitting a seat away on the other side of the sofa, and leaning toward him just enough to see the documents he withdrew. There was a note inside stating that the documents would be filed as soon as he signed, and several places flagged throughout where he'd need to put his name.

"Damn," she muttered and then scrubbed both hands over her face. "Is there an expiration time on those kinds of documents? If you sign now can they still be filed or do we have to have solicitors redraft the whole business and start over?"

Start over.

He had no idea what the answer to her question was, but he knew the answer he wanted. Start over. With her. They weren't divorced. They weren't the same people. Things could be different this time…

CHAPTER FIVE

"WHAT HAPPENED IN your past that you didn't want people to find out about?"

"Quinn, focus on the papers."

"I am."

"No, you're focusing on things that only mattered when we had a marriage to save. And you said you didn't want to get married again." She went to finally toss the contacts, but he'd swear it was to shut down the conversation.

And that was too bad. He wasn't ready; he'd waited years so she could give him more than a few minutes. "I don't. I married you. Yeah, you left, and we both thought we were divorced…"

"We are divorced."

"Until I put my name on these documents, we're still married." Quinn dropped them onto the coffee table and turned to face her, ignoring the hitch in his chest that came from her words. "Marrying you wasn't the wrong decision. Maybe I failed at being a husband in every regard, but marrying you wasn't wrong. You feel it too, or you and I would not have ended up on the floor together within seconds of being alone in a room. You still want me."

"Chemistry. As I said. And you said that was a goodbye or did you forget that too?"

"We have chemistry and a legally binding marriage. Unless you want to take it to court and let them decide." He couldn't focus on the goodbye bit. He'd said it at the time more from anger than because he'd thought it through.

"What could you possibly say in court to make people believe this is a real marriage? You and I haven't had a scrap of communication in years. You didn't know where I worked, you didn't know about my name change, you didn't even know I was back in the country." She flung her hands up, as if those sad facts won the argument and he was too simple to see it.

So quiet he could barely hear himself over his own pounding heart, Quinn answered, "I'd say I still love you."

For a second, he thought she was going to slug him. His words hung there in the air as those blue-green eyes narrowed and her nostrils flared.

Definitely going to do something to him.

Quinn waited, holding her gaze…

"Well, that's just perfect!" she finally shouted, throwing her arms toward the ceiling, her voice rising with every word. "You still love me. Great. That's *great*. Because it worked out so well last time. Not that I believe you. You've tarted your way across at least four continents on your leave over the last few years. Because it gets around, you know. News. Playboy Prince back at it, once unsaddled from his horrible bride. Of course, I'm sure you were thinking of me the whole time!"

"I'm not making excuses for seven years of perceived bachelorhood. You don't need to explain how you've spent that time either—and, for both our sakes, I beg you not to. It doesn't matter now." He said the words quietly enough that she had to stop her tirade to hear him. "You should know better than to believe everything you read in the gossip rags."

"So those pictures were just faked? No cover models?"

Words he'd said just to upset her on that first day had apparently hit their target. He gritted his teeth. *Stay on track.* What good could come from making her believe the worst of him when it wasn't true? "There's never been anyone else. Not in any way that counted. Not in any way that couldn't happen in public."

Her head fell back, eyes swiveled to the ceiling as she breathed out. It only lasted long enough to name it: relief. Long enough for her too, by the tension rocketing through her.

Relief to rage.

Her still lovely features twisted and, with a sound caught somewhere between a scream and a sob, she took three wide steps across the room and returned with the wrought iron poker which had been leaning beside the fireplace.

He tensed, ready to defend himself, even if the very idea that she'd actually attack him was so alien it made the world tilt.

She lifted the thing and brought it down with all her might on the glass-topped table where the unsigned divorce documents rested. Once. Twice. Again. Again. Punctuating each swing with a word either grunted or screamed. "I. Hate. This. *Table.*"

White spots in the shape of the poker appeared with each swing until finally a resounding crack announced a split in the top. He flinched and leaned back as she brought the iron rod down again.

Another smash shattered it, leaving the documents lying amongst the broken shards.

He made it up and around the table's remains as she shifted her attention to the metal base and brought the weapon down again. "I. Hate. This. Table. Hate. Hate. *Hate.*"

When she changed her swing, Quinn took the opening and shot out his left damaged hand, stopping her swing. The force of the impact sent a spike of pain spreading through what remained of his palm and up his arm.

The shock of hitting something living made her let go, and she froze on the spot, looking at him, looking at his hand. He flung the rod down and then swept her up in his still aching arms to track away from the coffee table carnage.

"What are you doing? Put me down!" She squirmed until he released her across the room, away from any shattered glass spray. Before she could get any distance, he locked his good hand around her wrist, and felt her fist ball.

The pit that had opened in him as he saw her destroy the coffee table began to make his guts swirl. "More violence? This is not you."

Anais was gentle. Tender-hearted. She didn't go on destructive rampages when upset. She got very quiet, she spent time alone. Sometimes she cried. She didn't break things.

At least this smashing spree was easier on his equilibrium than watching her cry had ever been, but he still felt the need to stop it. He raised his voice. "Stop fighting. I'm no danger."

"Every second I'm with you I'm in danger!"

Reactive words to make him back off. Part of him even wanted to, but the biggest thoughts echoing in his mind refused to let him leave.

She hadn't broken them. She'd just been the one to walk away from his mess.

"I could never be a danger to you," he said softly, holding her gaze, praying she actually heard him. He'd heard her—even if it'd taken nearly eight years if he counted their marriage.

He'd always known they'd been in trouble, but he'd also thought they'd have more time. He'd thought he'd be able to get her to stay until the tide turned, that something would happen, that opinions would change. Because they had been in trouble, but he'd still wanted her with every piece of him.

He still did. Yes, they'd changed. She was a doctor now. He was a man, not just walking around in a man's body. Surely the people wouldn't see them the same way.

"Let me go."

The demand came, and neither of them pretended it didn't mean more than a simple request to release her wrist.

"No," he said, keeping eye contact and his hold on her arm. "It was a mistake last time."

"I don't want to be your wife."

"I didn't want to go into the military. Or get divorced. Amazingly, both of those things worked out well for me. I'm not the same man I was, Anais. Tell me what you were afraid of."

"That's nothing you need to know anymore," she said through gritted teeth. "What I'm currently afraid of? Staying married to you. I don't want to be part of the PR parade that is being a princess. I hated it the first time, and this time it will only be worse."

She swung her arm up to her face and, with her free arm, grabbed his wrist in return. Without missing a beat, she turned out to the side, twisting his arm at the shoulder.

He wasn't ready for it, and the twist and sharp stab of pain made him let go of her wrist. Just as she'd wanted.

"I never fit. I could never fit or be accepted—it was futile. All I ever was, all I could ever be, was a stain on you and your family. That's still what I'd be."

Stepping away from him, she grabbed her bag and swung it over her shoulder, but paused when she looked at him, at the shock he could feel written on his face. She'd easily slipped his hold and, more importantly—she could've really hurt him if she'd wanted to. Did *Gray's Anatomy* include a section on self-defense and the best way to dislocate a shoulder? What, in God's name, had she been up in the States?

"You never fought for us, Quinn," she said, plucking his thoughts in his face. "You never fought for me. You never even met me on the damned battlefield. After you, I had to learn to fight for myself."

She was nearly at the door. Leaving a conversation she didn't want to be part of—something she'd probably learned from him. Fighting might make her stay. "Looks to me like you learned to hide yourself."

"I did that too." She swung the door open and looked back at him. "Do yourself and your whole family a favor. Sign the papers."

She didn't blink, and there was a warning in her stare: *get ready for a fight.*

"What are we doing here, Doc?" Ben asked, sounding tired already even though Quinn knew this was the first time during his stay at Almsford that he'd been to the gym. Physical therapists were required to ask every day but, since his attempted hanging, they hadn't been pushing anything. Not that he couldn't still be tired; emotional exhaustion was more insidious than the physical variety.

"What do you think we're doing?"

"Some kind of lesson on perseverance, I guess." The disgruntled tone at least sounded a little more energetic than it had seconds before.

Quinn parked the wheelchair where they could both watch an amputee patient using the parallel bars for stability while he walked on a new prosthesis under direction from a physical therapist.

"Nailed it," Quinn said.

"Not exactly the same situation," Ben said after spending a few brief seconds watching the man. "He's still got a functioning leg. I'm missing two."

"One and a half," Quinn corrected, fetched himself a chair and sat down beside Ben. "With a prosthetic on your longer leg, you could use crutches and get out of this chair. Then, after you got used to one, you could go for the other."

"Your wife feed you that line?"

"Gave me the literature. Why? Would you be more willing to hear it if it came from Rosalie? I'm sure she'd tell you the same, if you'd see her."

Ben eyed him sideways, "Don't make this harder. She deserves better and you'd feel the same way."

He was talking about his other injury, the one he didn't discuss directly. And, since he didn't, Quinn didn't tackle it head-on either. In a way, this not talking felt productive and safe, but he could see it being too indirect to deliver any results either. "There's a fix for everything, brother."

"You tell that whopper to your wife too?"

He didn't really want to talk about Anais, but Ben had brought her up twice. "Haven't exactly. Woman damned near broke my hand, and then my arm last night. Right after she obliterated my coffee table with a fireplace poker."

Ben's brows shot up. "Guess I'm lucky she didn't have a weapon handy yesterday when I called her a bad princess."

There was no containing his wince. "She wasn't a bad princess. She just never had a chance. Starting to think it was my fault too. Philip told me to clean it up. He meant to settle the divorce, make it official, but I don't want to."

"Because she didn't have a chance?"

"No. I don't know. I just can't wrap my head around the idea of letting her get away a second time." If they were doing this about Anais, he wasn't backing off Rosalie. "I never could let her go. Neither will Rosalie. If you keep on, you're sentencing her to a half-life. She'll never get over you, and you know it."

"She's stronger than you."

"Tell yourself lies, if that's what you've got to do," Quinn muttered. "She said I never fought for her. Don't know what irritates me more—the idea of it, or that she's right. I'm not making that same mistake again."

"Helen's going to be so happy to see us. You should've heard her when I called to say we were coming."

Anais checked the rearview as Mom spoke, noting the long string of cars still following all the way from her townhouse to the main street in Easton.

Security? Media? She didn't know who they were, just took a small amount of comfort in the distance between her back bumper and their front. All the while trying not to let on to Mom how nervous they made her. "It's good of her to be willing to open the shop on her day off."

"Are you worried about coming?"

Of course she'd noticed. Even with seven years of ocean between them, Mom had been able to read her through nothing but a phone line. Sometimes less. Sometimes she'd known when to call.

This was supposed to be a happy visit for Mom, and Anais didn't want to ruin it. "I'm glad we decided to come. It'll be nice to see everyone, and maybe Aunt Helen can help me peel away another layer of Anna and look more myself. It'll be nice to see me when I look in the mirror."

"That won't be a problem. At least with your hair. I don't know about your skin, though."

"She might have some tricks. People will have come to her about an overly orange experience before. But I'll exfoliate later. Always makes it fade faster."

Anna's look no longer served her, and might never serve her again—even if she truly needed it. If she couldn't get this marriage situation smoothly and quickly sorted out, she might need to run again. The thought shot a pang through her belly. What could she do then? Cut her hair off? Gain weight? Plastic surgery? Would Mom come too next time? Anais couldn't leave her behind again. Not now.

The small inner-city salon came into view; directly in front of the building was an empty parking place. Anais darted into it and parked before looking up and down the street to take inventory.

Cars lined both sides of the street, nowhere else to park. Maybe that would work in their favor—deter some of the vehicles following them.

They bundled out of the car and Anais waited for her mother to go into the salon ahead of her, then turned to track the progress of the vehicles, making mental note of the makes and colors.

One of them squeezed into a spot just after another car pulled out, but the other four picked up speed and headed uptown.

"Must have found a better headline than *Princess Visits Salon*," Mom said from beside her, arm coming around her waist. "Well, most of them. That one black car probably hasn't heard about whatever is happening yet."

She was trying to help, and that defeated the whole point of Anais's plan to give her mother a good day with her sister and friends, since moving in with Anais had separated them. To take her mind off their uncertain future, and how that might increase the distance between them if they were forced to leave. "Go say hi to Aunt Helen. She's probably about to explode in a shower of fabulous glitter by now."

They'd no sooner stepped inside and away from the door than Anais heard a click behind her and a spike of fear had her spinning to face the danger. A pink-smocked woman she didn't recognize had locked the door. "To keep them cameras out, Princess."

The uniform marked her as an employee, which abated Anais's alarm a little. She really had to do better if she wanted Mom to have a good day. "Thank you, that's a good idea. Don't... I'm not really a princess. It's all a mistake. Please call me Anais."

She'd pretend the door locking would keep everyone out, not just the lawful people who wouldn't break through the wide picture window upon which the salon name had been painted.

Anais focused again through the window on the black sedan that had followed them; the window was rolled down, and she half expected to see Quinn sitting there, but she saw a man in a black suit instead, with an earpiece. He nodded once to her across the way, and the darkened window rolled back up.

Royal Security.

Great. Now the King had gotten involved. Was that better than cameras or worse?

Worse, she decided. It validated the situation somehow. Made Quinn's cooperation seem less likely.

A flurry of greetings broke in on her thoughts and before long she'd been ushered out of her jacket, into hugs, and finally a spinning chair, and some nice person muted the still running television on the wall behind her. Although Easton had never fit her either, there was a homey feeling to her aunt's salon—somewhere she'd safely spent hours with her nose in books and where no one had made fun or bullied the local Poindexter.

Work, card games with her friends; Mom was there so much that Anais was practically related to their core group—they all thought she was brilliant, and had been proud of her marriage. People she'd let down in many ways—some they still didn't know about and wouldn't, so long as those pictures stayed private.

She almost felt as if she belonged there, a feeling she'd been looking for when she'd set her sights and non-existent seduction skills on Wayne Ratliffe. The idea had been: community acceptance through the coolest guy in the neighborhood. Get him to like her; the rest would fall in line.

It was everything past the idea that had gone wrong. Her teenage brain had no execution skills. Pretending to be cool meant drinking the alcohol he'd given her. Two drinks in, making out sounded like winning. Three drinks in, he'd convinced her that girls who took pride in their bodies shared them with boyfriends… And then the pictures…

She should be paying attention to what they were saying.

She felt Mom's gaze before she saw it as Mom launched in with the talking Anais was failing to do. "Strip out the brunette…dye the proper shade back if needed…blah-blah-blah…spray tan removal…"

Their excitement redirected easily enough, Anais settled in, with tired but genuine smiles dutifully mustered.

Helen spun her so that she could watch the window through the mirror in front of her, and got to work, whisking a protective cape around her and snagging a bowl of foul-smelling chemicals with an applicator.

No book today; she could either fixate on her past stupidity, stare paranoid out the window or listen.

Or she could think about Quinn, since they were chatting about him now.

It had been two days since she'd seen him and Hulk-smashed his coffee table. The urge to break it, or throw it off the perfect balcony, had been with her every day, starting about the fourth month of their marriage—when they'd been gifted with the keys. Prior to that, they'd lived in a small flat near the country's best university—and social strata—a scholarship had granted her access to, and had come to the capital on the weekends to try and get his family used to her and for her to take some solace with her mom.

Someone else had bought the penthouse.

Someone else had decorated it.

Someone who probably thought a microbiology major would want obsessively modern tastes, which had instead shocked her system. But their whole marriage had been a shock to her system. And they'd spent so much time in the bedroom, she'd convinced herself that the rest of the apartment didn't matter. Just like she'd originally bought Quinn's notion that the rest of the world didn't matter. Until it began to matter. Until she'd started seeing glimpses of Wayne. Until Wayne had made clear it was still true—that she'd never belong with Quinn any more than she'd belonged in Easton.

She still didn't know whether or not she'd actually seen him early on, or if it had just been her subconscious worrying her about that part of her past she'd been ignoring, that part which would come up and derail them. Corrachlean had remained a monarchy, steeped in traditional values through the centuries. It was a quaint culture that embraced certain modern notions—like equality—while still clinging to old values. A super-common princess raised by a single, never-married woman, who hadn't even a father named on her birth certificate, was impossible to accept, even without adding low-class nudies.

And Anais couldn't even make an excuse for it—at least not one that made her seem less pathetic.

They could never accept her and she still so desperately wanted them to.

Even Quinn wouldn't if he found out. He accepted her as she was, or as he thought her to be: sensible, with good judgment, highly intelligent—*brutally intelligent,* he'd once called her as a compliment. He loved that about her. Her act of extreme stupidity would counter that argument very effectively, even without introducing jealousy into the mix.

"Anais…"

Her mother's voice broke in as her chair began to spin, and soon she was looking at Quinn in full regalia on the television while one of the women scrambled to find the remote they'd just had moments ago, and a chill shot through her.

"Is he doing it?" Mom asked just as the volume returned and TV Quinn stopped nodding and waving and started to speak.

"I don't know. I hope so."

"Ladies and gentlemen, thank you for coming today."

Quinn stood at a podium in front of a sea of reporters, cameras rolling and, with a patience she couldn't believe he possessed, waited for them to get serious footage. She'd seen nothing of him on film—nothing past the grainy night shot of her giving him the documents for Ben.

He wore such a grave expression; for a moment she thought he was going to announce something serious about the King. The royals were always loved by the media—

except for her—but she hadn't seen any recent footage of the King, come to think of it.

But the Playboy Prince wasn't smiling. Not joking. Not charming them into letting him get away with murder.

"Today I want to speak to you about my wife, Dr. Anais Hayes or, as she's been known since returning to Corrachlean, Dr. Anna Kincaid. I know you're shocked, and really we were both surprised to find out the dissolution of our marriage had never been finalized. But it was a happy surprise."

Her anxiety beast reared up in her belly and started chewing.

"Oh, sweet mercy, don't do this, Quinn," Anais whispered, and only remembered she stood in public with foil in her hair when Mom's hand found hers and made her fingers release the knot she'd twisted her protective cape into.

"What's he doing?" Mom asked, the question whispered.

"He's…" Public. They were in public. Even if it were just Mom, Aunt Helen, and a couple of Mom's friends. She could trust family to keep things quiet, but maybe spilling any secrets in front of friends—no matter how close—wasn't the best idea.

She tried to force a placid air. "I don't know what he's doing. He didn't tell me he was having a press conference."

"Since we last saw Anais she's been in the United States. She took all the pain that came from our parting and channeled it. Made it through medical school with astounding grades—in keeping with the way she tackled university—and over the course of her training specialized in helping those who have served our country and paid the price with their bodies. I can't think of a more honorable, a more noble mission to dedicate her life to. I'm very proud of her."

Dammit.

"He's right," Aunt Helen said, and Anais couldn't argue because…what could she say? *I made a series of decisions that led to him losing his fingers; the least I could do was help others who suffered a similar fate?*

Over the years, his official royal uniform had been remade to fit his broadening frame, and in that time he'd really learned how to wear it. He looked more comfortable in it than she remembered and, even without the decorative epaulettes, his shoulders were broad and square beneath the tailored lines.

"I want to be clear now. The divorce was never finalized because of my inaction. She signed where she was told to sign, and I assumed that someone took care of those things for me and never checked in when I was home on leave. We've never had a divorce, and we're not going to have one now. I'm asking you to give us the space we need to fit our lives back together. I'll do whatever I need to protect her. I came home to fulfill my duty to my family, and she is my family, so I'm starting with my wife. If we have to leave Corrachlean to have any kind of peace together, to have the family we were always meant to have, we'll leave. I don't want that to happen."

"Did he just threaten to abdicate?" Mom asked, alarm evident, and three other sets of eyes swiveled to Anais.

"He's not going to be King," Anais murmured, even though she heard his intention as clearly. "He can't abdicate, but I think maybe he threatened to renounce his title."

Why in the name of heaven would he do that?

He seemed done talking, and once again stood stoically for the cameras, waiting.

Then the questions began…

CHAPTER SIX

AFTER THE PRESS conference Quinn changed and nicked a car from the palace garage. Forgoing a driver, he followed his GPS to Anais's town home.

Nice, quiet, upper middle class neighborhood. The late summer sunshine filtered through the leaves on the tree-lined street, one broad beam of light illuminating a parking place directly in front of her home. His opening gambit in the fight she'd threatened had felt right at the time but, going to face her now, his mind seemed some insane cocktail of worry, pessimism, and straight-up giddiness.

Fortune favored the brave, but he had no idea what it did with the inappropriately giddy. No man should be excited to fight with the woman he loved, but the other evening he'd felt closer to Anais than he had during their whole marriage. It was hard not to look forward to that kind of fire.

He parked the understated black sedan and hurried to her door. The street was quiet and more or less empty, aside from a woman walking her dog down the opposite side. The press seemed to have listened to his request—at least for now. No cars had followed him and he could see no cameras camped at her door.

He rang the bell and slipped a hand into his pocket, feeling the weight of the velvet box he'd retrieved from the crate tucked in there.

The ring she might not accept.

Probably wouldn't accept.

Might even smash with whatever weapon she had handy...

His pulse increased the longer he stood there. Just stick to the plan. Tell her they were staying married. Explain his plan to seduce the press. Tell her...

Still no one answered the door. He pressed the bell again.

Maybe she'd gone. Fled the country already. Had she had time for that since his announcement?

As he reached for the bell again, the door cracked open. Eyes that had once no doubt been the exact blue-green shade of Anais's found him, paler but distinctive enough to recognize the mother-in-law he hadn't seen in years.

"Sharon. Hello. Is...she here?"

"She's upstairs." No greeting, but she did let him inside. "She went to bed with a headache, but said to send you up if you came by."

Expecting him. Perhaps lying in wait with a fireplace poker...

The door closed behind him and she took a moment to engage the locks, something he was thankful to hear as he'd already started up the stairs.

"Last door," Sharon called after him. "Don't drive her away again, Quinton Corlow. She needs a home. She was happy here the past month."

He stopped midflight and looked back down at her, nodding because he didn't know what to say. But she had already turned and picked up a book she'd obviously been reading before he rang the bell, and sat on one end of the sofa.

From his position, he could see downstairs well enough to realize the stark difference in style between it and the penthouse. Bookshelves everywhere, loaded sometimes two rows deep with books. Furniture he could best describe as fluffy. Comfortable and welcoming, and...not why he was there. Later. He'd keep it in mind later when they looked for alternate housing to the penthouse. Or maybe just lived here... He wanted her to be happy in her home, and the penthouse had obviously failed in that.

Last door upstairs, he reminded himself, and completed the climb.

Stick to the plan.

The white panel door stood silently where indicated, no signs of movement beyond. No light below the door, and it was still daylight. But she was in there. He could feel her inside.

Taking a chance, he bypassed knocking, and instead peeked inside as quietly as the door would allow. Anais lay atop the blankets, eyes closed. Asleep?

The creak of the door opening brought Anais fully awake, "Mom?" The word came out before she'd even gotten her eyes fully open.

Quinn slipped into the room and faced her. Since his press conference, he'd changed back into the fatigues he'd been wearing most of the time when not in full royal regalia. "Sharon said you weren't feeling well. Has your head improved?"

"Not entirely. But it doesn't feel like my skull is being cleaved in two right now. Are you going to make it worse?" She stood up; it felt like the kind of conversation she'd be better able to handle on her feet, and with some light. She switched on the bedside lamp.

"Your hair..."

The wonder in his voice had her looking at him again. As she'd turned to the lamp, he'd crossed to her and now stood less than a foot away, his broken hand suddenly cupping her jaw. While she'd expected him to come by, she'd been unable to come up with a way to handle this thing he'd thrown at her. Now, with his hand on her face and the way his eyes searched her every feature, the pull of him further scrambled her thoughts.

"It's you. Finally." He swallowed hard, brows pressed too sharply together; he almost looked in pain, as if he'd just lost her, as if he couldn't bear to blink and risk her disappearing. The hand cupping her jaw stayed, but his free hand slid into her hair and smoothed the locks between his fingers. He finally looked from her face to the strand to watch the play of the color in the light. "It's really close. A little lighter than normal, like you've been at the beach."

The words, so at odds with the reverence and pain in his face, yanked her back into herself. "Aunt Helen stripped out the brunette today. Probably took a little extra color with it..."

"You're beautiful." A reverent whisper. The heat from his hand on her cheek left a fiery trail down her neck and over the skin bared by the strappy tank top she'd worn for sleep. His eyes followed his hand over her shoulder, then over her chest, concealed by the thin material she wore.

Beautiful, he'd said—the word, his voice, and his eyes said the same. He looked at her with an intensity and longing that twisted at her insides. She drew closer.

"Your skin is so soft."

Her palms ached and she rested them against his chest, felt the muscle bunch and tighten under her touch, and slid them higher toward his neck, just to feel his skin under her aching hands.

Sweet mercy, what was she doing?

She should move away right now. Take him to another room. She'd just wanted some privacy to talk when she'd told Mom to send him up, to keep her from being dragged further into this mess.

"In the desert, in the heat, everything felt sharp." He still stroked up and down her arms, speaking so quietly she wasn't even sure he knew he was speaking. "The wind would come and the sand felt like a million tiny knives. I liked to think about soft things, soothe myself with memories..."

In the wake of his hands, that dizzying tingle returned,

following his fingers and spreading out from them like an epicenter for some heart earthquake. Head sparkles and feet like lead came from the worshipful things he said.

"I could never remember anything softer than your skin. Could spend infinity stroking your skin."

He leaned forward and she lost all will to resist as his lips touched her shoulder—softness framed by the delicious scrape of the day's beard, scrubbing her mind.

He didn't kiss—there was no kissing—time stretched out as he simply stroked his warm, full lips feather-light over her shoulder, into the curve of her neck, then up into the hair behind her ear.

"You belong with me," he murmured, arms sliding around to bring her fully against him. "And I belong with you."

Yes.

Warmth rolled through her. It was like a drug. He was like a drug.

Her cheek rested against the center of his chest and she leaned against him as he stayed, head curled down, so that his every word was spoken into her skin, like a brand she'd never be able to scrub off.

"I know how to make it work this time. I know how to make them listen, make them love you too. I have a plan."

If he'd thrown her into Arctic tides off the northern coast he couldn't have surpassed the shock that lanced through her.

He was doing it again! Distraction. Distraction and sex and sweet words, and she fell for it every cursed time.

She jolted back, an accusing finger jabbing his way to convey the words stuck in her throat.

"Easy now."

"I'm not a horse!" she blurted out, possibly the dumbest thing she'd ever said in anger. Which was *his* fault too. Touching him never did anything good for her cognition. "Is this part of your plan? *Oh, Anais, you're so beautiful...*"

Two more big steps backward gave her more room to breathe, to think, but Quinn seemed to be amused more than anything. Amused and...exhilarated.

But it passed quickly.

"No." With the one word, the silk fell from his tone, along with the excited light in his eyes. "I have a publicity plan. They listened today. They're not loitering at your door. They didn't follow me here. They're listening. Our situation has changed."

Now she remembered what she'd gone to sleep to try and forget—his ridiculous press conference where he'd tried to make the people like her by telling them she was a doctor. "You threatened to renounce your title. That's why they're listening. They have to see how serious you are before calling your bluff. That'll take them at least a day. A week if you're lucky."

"You say that like it was an empty threat."

"You know it was empty. You're not going to follow through on that. You want to be here or you'd still be serving. Whatever you just said about soothing memories of softness. You didn't leave the military after your injury, and I know they would have offered it to you."

"We could argue this all day and you'd still be wrong." He waved a hand. "That's not what I was talking about. Our situation is different because you're different. You're accomplished, not just a common girl the daft Prince fell for. And there's nothing people like better than a fairy tale. All we have to do is give them the fairy tale, Cinderella. Do some appearances..."

"Some appearances? You're talking about more than appearances!"

"We'll go through with The Sip; I've already got someone organizing the invitation lottery on that since the people complained about missing it the first time. They'll eat it up."

"Of course they complained. It's Corrachlean's centuries-old royal engagement traditional party, and everyone loves free-flowing mead and bad decision-making." She grunted when her head throbbed again.

"Not you."

"No, not me," she replied.

"And then we'll have the lavish wedding every Cinderella would dream of." He crossed to her again and leaned past her to pick up a bottle of pain relievers. "When did you last take one?"

"Too recently, even though they're clearly worthless." She took a breath, smelled only him, and then took another couple of steps away from him in the other direction so she could try and maintain some semblance of sense. "I don't want this."

"And I don't want a divorce. Besides, I don't believe you. You were right there with me moments ago. You were right there with me on your office floor. It's still there. We're not going to be the first divorce in the history of the royal family. You wanted me to fight for you? This is me fighting for you."

Her cheeks burned—like she needed to be reminded how easy he could have her. She stammered, "It's too late for grand gestures."

"I don't accept that."

"Because you say it's not? I can't go back to that unforgiving spotlight. I don't want to be a freaking princess—"

"What's the alternative?" he cut in. "Tell me what your plan was after our faulty divorce was discovered. Just to wait for the fervor to die down? I tried that once; you lost your mind. You already are *a freaking* princess, in the most literal sense. Right now. That's who you are. Princess Anais Corlow, not Hayes, and sure as hell not Kincaid."

"Legally, I'm Dr. Anna Kincaid."

"Actually, you're not. Philip doesn't have the authority to unilaterally rename a princess and strip her of her title. It's invalid, like those unsigned divorce documents."

Shock that she hadn't considered that sent her scrambling. "Fine! Whatever. I don't have a plan for any of this. You just threw it at me on live TV. I've been trying to figure out how to make this go away; you're just making it worse."

"I could make it much worse."

The quietly delivered statement made her breath catch. That was a threat. By this point in her life she knew a threat when she heard one, and that was a threat. She didn't even have to take the coldness of his tone into consideration, or the way his deep gray eyes hardened over like ice sheets blowing in from the North Sea. "What are you saying?"

"I'm saying the press listened to me today. We can give them the fairy tale, or I can give them my heartbreak. How long do you think it will take to die down if I tell them I came home from a war zone to this, that you led me on then broke my heart again?"

She wobbled and staggered backwards until the wall stopped her. Quinn reached for her, but she'd stopped before he could cross the distance to her.

"That's you fighting for me, or just with me? I think I like the old Quinn better; at least he wasn't...horrible." Old Quinn joked, used happy distractions, in retrospect. This Quinn? She didn't know him.

"I am fighting for us."

"By lying and manipulating people? You know that's not what happened."

"I just told them we weren't getting divorced and how happy that made me. Two true things."

"You're blackmailing me now? I already have one blackmailer; I don't need two!"

A flash of fire in his eyes alerted her to the words that had flown from her mouth. His long stride ate up the distance between them and his hands on her shoulders kept her facing him, fingers biting into her shoulders enough to trigger an ache, which should've blocked out that damnable tingling, but didn't. "You have a blackmailer?"

She shook her head immediately, desperate for some

way to rewind that accidental confession. "No. Kind of. I did have."

"You had a blackmailer?"

"And, you know, I could have two if you're joining the ranks." She laughed bitterly as she sifted through anything she could say to salvage this.

Nothing could put that genie back into the bottle. But maybe it would tell him exactly how unacceptable she'd be as a royal if the pictures were ever leaked.

"Blackmailed over what, Anais? By whom?" The way he looked at her made it impossible to look away.

"I have nude photos. Out there. Someone else...has them." The words came out broken, and just having to say them made her feel broken. "You can't have those and be a princess without getting a blackmailer. That's just a little fact of life I learned about ten months after we eloped. There's no way to spin that into a fairy tale. Cinderella only had to overcome being the help. Not being incredibly stupid one regrettable night."

"Ten months?" he repeated, his brow pinching as the cogs started clicking into place.

"Yes. Ten months. And for a whole month I tried." The air had gone thin; she breathed too hard and had to swivel her eyes upward to keep the stinging tears from falling. "Never mind. Just accept that I have this, and he will come back. Now that you've done this, he'll come back. He's... He's coming back."

"Someone you were dating?" He wasn't backing off.

"No. Kind of. I was a teenager. He was just a guy in my neighborhood."

That answer took away some of the tension from his frame. "And?"

"And what?" She ducked from beneath his clamping hands, and darted across the room again. "He found me after we were married and demanded money or he'd sell the photos; he carried a huge grudge over some other things, and I didn't know how to make him go away. At first I told him it would take me a while to get the money—and, considering the amount he wanted, he accepted that. I tried to work out how to fix it, and how to tell you, and I tried so many times, but it never worked. So, I left. Okay? I removed myself so at least if he did come out with them you'd be blameless. Because what could you do then? I'd already be gone and my leaving would've been good news to the people."

Despite the wild look in his eyes, Quinn didn't chase her this time—her first nod to hope. He got it, or he was getting it. "You never told me any of this."

"I tried. Every time I brought up the terrible public outcry against my very existence, you'd change the subject or we'd end up naked."

"Quinn, I'm being blackmailed," he said. "That's all you had to say to stop my coping mechanisms."

"Oh, sure." She stilled, the spike drilling down into the top of her head jabbing again. "Because that's the way to make your new husband eager to feel helpful and protective. We *didn't talk* about things. We didn't. We played, we flirted, we teased, and we spent more time naked than we spent clothed together."

"That's an exaggeration."

"It doesn't feel like one."

He stopped the question with a wave of his hand. "Just give me his name. Where does he live?"

"Like we've been pen pals all this time? I don't know where he is and won't until he comes at me again. I don't even know why he never sold the photos after I left without paying him. That whole first year away, I expected it to show up on my Internet alerts but it never did."

Quinn crossed to her desk, picked up a pad and pen from the tidy top, and handed it to her. "Write down his name, approximate age, where he used to live, whatever you remember."

"What are you going to do?" She took the pad, but didn't yet start writing.

"I'm going to fight for my wife. You don't need details, unless you're worried I might hurt him."

"I don't care if you hurt him." She wrote Wayne Ratliffe's name, the address of his former dingy apartment around the corner to where she'd grown up, lingered briefly over the five-year age difference between them... Then handed the pad back to Quinn, unsure how to feel about it. He hadn't gotten it yet; maybe he still needed to work through it. Until then, Quinn had access to people to handle these sorts of situations, she didn't, and it would serve him and the family if this didn't come out.

Even if those weren't legit reasons to accept his help, it would do her sanity good—that prickling feeling that Wayne was waiting just around every corner had resurfaced the instant she'd learned they were still married and the world knew it.

Quinn ripped the top sheet off and set the pad back on the desk, then fished a small box from his pocket and set it on top of the paper.

Without asking or opening the box, she knew.

Engagement ring.

Another sinking in her stomach she'd have to ignore.

CHAPTER SEVEN

"ANAIS, HONEY, HE'S HERE, and he's brought the whole brigade with him."

Anais sucked in a deep breath and rose from the least comfortable and least wrinkle-inducing chair in her living room, and smoothed her hands over the pretty white eyelet lace dress she'd purchased yesterday for today's outing with Quinn. "Do I look okay? I feel silly, wearing such a dress for a walk in the park."

"You always look beautiful, and the sandals make it a little more sensible."

"All that's missing is a big floppy hat and oversized glasses," she joked and leaned over to hug the worry out of her mother.

The squeeze she got in return bolstered her courage. It had only taken three days of constantly weighing Quinn's proposal to decide there were more pros than cons. Mom's worry was what finally made her come around. She couldn't run again. Mom deserved to have her and her sister in her life. If the heart condition had frightened Anais enough to go to Philip for help, she'd find the courage to do whatever she had to do to stay.

"You don't have to do anything you don't want to do. We can leave. Any country would be lucky to have a talented, caring doctor come to them."

"I know, Mom." She kissed her mother's cheek, glad

she'd kept her big list of reasons to herself. Mom's heart reacted badly to stress; the situation already worried her enough she'd been popping in and out of rhythm since the press first showed up on their doorstep.

It would all be worth it to stay and keep her healthy; no matter what Mom said about leaving together, this was her home.

As long as Quinn could take care of Wayne.

"It's going to be okay. Things might still change, but you know Quinn's never been cruel to me. I'm going to play it by ear. You're not going to have to leave home or Aunt Helen. Try not to worry, okay?"

She made some sound that both affirmed her intention to not worry while highlighting her disbelief that Anais thought it was possible not to.

The bell rang, Anais smoothed her hands over the cheerful princess dress again, and paused by the entrance table to eye the velvet box there. She still hadn't opened it, and couldn't even say why. After grabbing a small matching handbag, she carefully picked up the box as if it were rigged to explode, put it into her bag, and stepped out of the house and into Quinn.

Without missing a beat, he kissed her cheek and took her hand in his left, the usual way they'd held hands. "You look beautiful. I think I'm underdressed."

Threats last time, charm today. And she'd ignore the heart flip that happened when he'd kissed her. The threat didn't need to be forgotten; it was a reminder why she had to go with the flow until he caught up with her on the only sensible, peaceful way their lives could go. The one where *he* dumped *her* this time, and the media lost interest.

She stepped back far enough to get a look at him. The gray slacks he wore were obviously made for the man, crisp and lightweight but still tailored. His white button-down sat open at the collar, revealing the thick masculine neck that…said as much about his transition from boy to man as anything could. He'd gone from slim and lithe to broad and strong, and the definition in his neck made it clear to her how the rest of his body would reflect this strength.

"You look great." She didn't comment on his freshly shaved jaw, the curls starting in the thick brown hair that had grown out of the neat military cut he would have worn since enlisting. Ignore that too; she didn't need reminding of the boyish, carefree fop she'd always delighted in running her fingers through.

"Somehow that didn't sound like a compliment," he murmured, then looked at their joined hands, paused a beat, a measuring slant to his brow, then let go with his damaged hand and switched sides to link five fingers with her own.

"Why did you just switch sides?"

He squeezed her fingers with his whole hand and gave a little tug toward the cars, answering quietly. "It looks better, draws attention away from the imperfect, messy parts. And I thought you might prefer it."

"You seriously think I feel revulsion for your injury?" She could buy him wanting things to appear perfect—a walk through the city's largest green space on a sunny summer afternoon would yield photos of some kind—but his suggestion she'd feel disdain over his missing fingers made her stomach turn heavy and she couldn't keep the annoyance at bay. "I work with amputees—"

"I didn't soften the situation for you when I told you," he cut in, his voice staying low despite there being no one near enough to hear them. She had to remind herself he'd probably never considered how she'd faced his injury. He continued when they'd settled in the back seat, "I did for everyone else. Only you, me and Ben know how that went. The rest of the world, including the current and future king, believe the fingers cleanly came off and we just had to bandage it up and carry on."

Talking about it hurt. So did thinking about it.

Unable to stop herself, Anais reached for his left hand

and clasped it in both of hers, suddenly needing him to really know that the only negative she felt about it was that he'd gone through it and that her ring had probably made it worse. "You don't trust me, so why did you tell me a truth you don't want known?"

"Anger." He turned his hand in hers and gripped, strong but not hard, dexterous control as good as she could hope for anyone. "You were too calm, and inside I was boiling."

She'd looked calm? Every part of her had been shaking, but maybe fear and regret could be hidden better than rage. Arguing her state at the time wouldn't do anything for them, so she just let silence fall as he gave orders to the driver and the black sedan entourage pulled onto the quiet street.

He'd hurt, and he'd wanted to hurt her too so he'd lashed out, lending weight to the notion he could strike at her again if she refused him now.

Where could this kind of marriage leave them in ten years? After children? After their volatile passion had run its course?

There'd been no one since him, and he'd said the same. Seven years of celibacy was a long time. Felt like some version of love, maybe…if he truly could become involved, if he was going to help with Wayne because he wanted her safe more than the idea of it ruining his plan to undo that black mark that divorce left on his royal record.

She retrieved the ring from her handbag and handed the box to him. "Should I wear this?"

"Do you like it?" Quinn asked, a tone in his voice hinting how important it was for her to say yes. "If you'd prefer a different ring…we can make that happen."

"I haven't looked at it," she admitted, keeping her hand flat for him with the box sitting on her palm until he took it.

Whatever he thought about that, he opened the box and presented the ring to her.

Anais had expected ostentatious, to feel self-conscious about the size of the stone—Quinn's way always involved big gestures—but she hadn't expected to *feel*. Or the way the air became so thin.

She hadn't expected a blue-green stone, hadn't even known such a stone existed. Large, yes, but not horrifying. And there were two additional but smaller princess-cut diamonds flanking it in a platinum band so delicate it didn't look strong enough to support the gems.

Heartbreakingly beautiful.

"It matches your eyes," he offered softly, and the ring bomb went off as he plucked it from the velvet pillows and slid it onto her finger.

Eyes burning, she took a slow breath then clamped her mouth shut to stop her lower lip trembling.

A beautiful ring shouldn't make this harder; she wasn't that person. She'd never cared about that stuff.

Another breath as she felt her hand fist, keeping the ring from moving, keeping her from gazing at it as if she were star-struck. "Sapphire?"

Please be a sapphire.

"Alexandrite."

A stone she hadn't even heard of. Probably magnificently rare and jimmied off some ancient crown or necklace, one bit of the family jewels to show how serious he was.

"New?"

"Seven years old." He turned her chin toward him, leaned in and kissed her mouth lightly; again her lip trembled. "Can I infer you like it?"

"Seven years?"

"It was an anniversary present."

Pow.

"It's beautiful." She swallowed, cursing herself for how dejected she sounded over being given a magnificent ring.

He'd kept it the whole time. He'd picked it out when they were still together. An engagement ring, for the engagement they'd never had.

Damn him.

The weight of it all drowned out everything ricocheting through her mind, and Quinn let her drift into silence until they got to the park. He kept her hand; his thumb brushed her finger, slightly moving the ring this way and that, playing havoc with her emotions.

No threats, just charm, sweetness and romance. She'd almost prefer the angry man who'd trapped her into this arrangement to this shimmer of who she'd fallen so hard for that she'd let herself live in the fantasy that she could ever fit into his world. She'd found a place in the medical world, more than she'd ever found anywhere, including where she'd grown up and those first seventeen years of never fitting in.

The car pulled into the park and Quinn helped her from the back. Taking his place again on her left where he could hold her ringed hand in his whole hand, guiding her down a cobblestone path through the trees ringing a large meadow and central pond.

The security detail walked several meters behind, close enough to respond quickly in case of emergency, but far enough for a modicum of privacy. About the same distance ahead of them, another couple walked, blissfully unaware through the cool afternoon shade of the silver birch trees.

"Have you had any luck tracking down Wayne?" She opted for a shorthand, normalized manner to ask about the bane of her adult existence. The horrified delight she still felt from the ring needed countering.

"Yes, but I haven't met with him yet," Quinn answered, his voice so quiet and sedate she had to look at him to work out whether to attach positive or negative meaning to his words.

Nothing. Just calm.

"Have you contacted him?"

"Not yet." He released her hand, stepped around to the side he preferred and wrapped his arm around her waist instead, anchoring her to him.

In the cool shade, his body pressed heat against her skin.

No, not heat. Warmth. A sense of security despite the lack of movement on Wayne. "Why not?"

"He's not in a position to cause damage right now. We have some time."

"How do you know?"

"He's incarcerated," Quinn answered, the calm in his voice fracturing briefly with a note of disdain. "Solitary confinement for another few days. He attacked a guard."

Jail? That shouldn't shock her. Blackmail wasn't the man's only crime. "What did the police get him for?"

Giving a minor alcohol?

Inappropriate contact with a minor?

Talking a drunken teen into nudie shots?

Even though Anais knew she was smart, she'd still had her thinking corrupted by the desire to belong somewhere... to someone. So her crime was worse than other girls he'd just tricked. She'd known better and done it anyway.

"I'm having his record sent over tonight but, with what I've learned, he sounds like a great guy. Do me a favor and don't tell me how you ever dated with someone like that."

Dated. They'd never dated. The implication caused her to bristle, even though she was supposed to want Quinn to be coming to exactly this kind of conclusion—the one that would lead to him thinking her not suitable for the royal family.

This was her opening to tell him the truth—pathetic and tired after a childhood of bullying and verbal abuse, she'd walked herself right off the cliff and was still falling. To point out the way it mirrored her decision-making when she and Quinn had eloped. Willful ignorance, ridiculous self-deception.

"We've all been stupid teenagers once."

The words refused to come.

"Once I know what he's been convicted of, and if there has been any previous incarceration, I'll know how to approach him."

All sensible. And surprisingly proactive, but too new a character trait to trust. "Please keep me in the loop. I need to be involved in this. To know what's going on."

"I'm handling it." He didn't sound angry, even leaned over to brush his lips against her temple. The couple ahead of them had finally noticed who walked behind them and now had a cellphone out. "You wanted me to help with it before."

"I did. I do," she whispered, smiling at the couple, still several meters away, then leaned up to kiss his cheek in return. Because it felt as if he'd kissed her head as part of his PR thing. "I trust you to handle it. It's just been eating at me for so long; being afraid of it, of him, is hard-wired."

The quiet confession earned her a longer look, a spike of irritation in his eyes. "I'll fix it. I'm used to storming barriers." This should be seen as a romantic walk with sweet touches, and she really hoped the cameras didn't pick up the quiet, tense conversation. All they needed was a video to deal with.

Another group of people approached from the park's other path, and the couple who'd been filming stepped to the side to allow them to pass.

With the path about to become narrower, Anais pressed against him, trying to edge Quinn off the walk with her to make way, but his arm firmed at her waist and he held her to the center.

"We need to move," she whispered, and he shook his head, lifting the whole hand he'd earlier freed and waved at the people.

The group stepped off the path, and Quinn continued forward. "People are used to a kind of deference, and even if it feels strange to me too it's tradition and I try to keep it up. You'll have to get used to things again."

"It feels rude," she muttered, her smile faltering for the first time since they'd reached the wide open public space. "I'm no different to them. I think putting myself into that false headspace is part of why I struggled so much with the title. I hate being called Princess."

"Next time we'll move to the side, and you'll see what happens. The smoothest way of handling things is the traditional route here, doing what people expect. Like this. Courting. The Sip. The wedding."

"It's not really a wedding. We're still married."

"But we never had a proper wedding. This will be a fresh start for us. Starting over, and doing it how we should've before. It's a wedding."

Pick your battles, dummy.

As the path opened to a wide meadow, he steered them to the east where she now saw a small table and servers hovered nearby. Lunch in the park. Let it never be said he didn't know how to put on a show. Maybe he was right.

"Shouldn't fairy tales have picnics on the ground with red gingham blankets?"

"We can sit on the ground if you want, but you're the one in the white dress." The charm and smile returned. "Ben met with the designers for a prosthesis this week. Even met with the vascular surgeon. Hasn't agreed to surgery, but he's listening."

"How did you manage it?" She went with the subject change. Ben was her patient too and she'd been failing to get him to consider a prosthesis for a month. "Did he hit you with RoboCop jokes?"

He pulled out her chair. "He hit me with much worse. I just have better ammunition to fight back."

The afternoon sun warmed her shoulders and she let her eyes track over the park as he settled opposite her and the servers began to fuss, filling glasses with juice and water, presenting dishes of fruit, cheese, and little meat pastries. No wine. He remembered that too.

More sweetness and consideration. Fighting for Ben. Fighting for her?

Looking at him got hard.

She shifted her gaze toward the pond and, set against the green water, maybe thirty meters from where they sat, he stood.

A shock of ice shot through her and she heard Quinn urgently saying her name.

Lanky, tall, gaunt of face, shaggy brown hair, and a deep corded scar across his right cheek.

It was happening.

A glass of water shot off the table and Anais saw it, but barely had enough control of her shaking hands to latch on to Quinn's closest arm. "It's him."

Quinn let her glass fall, gaze fixed on Anais's bloodless face. Even her forever pink lips looked like chalk, but the violent tremble in her hands on his arm just made it worse.

Her fear summoned his; needles of awareness assaulted the back of his neck and he felt himself tensing, readying for a fight.

She'd said *him*.

"Him?" he echoed, following her gaze to a man loitering some distance away.

Ratliffe?

Couldn't be. He was rotting in solitary in prison an hour from the capital as of two hours ago.

Quinn forced himself to relax and waved off the approaching security team. He didn't even know what Ratliffe looked like yet but, even if he had, he was too distant to see much aside from generalities. Tall. Overly thin. In need of a haircut, a shave, and a tee shirt without a hole in it.

"It's him," she said again, then looked at him, then back at the security people. Quinn shook his head at them again. "How did he know we'd be here?"

"It's not him, Anais." Shifting from fighting mode to being gently protective, he disengaged her clutching hands to take them both in his own. "He's in solitary, remember? That's not him."

"It's him."

The fear rolling off her made him doubt for a few seconds but, unless the man was an escape artist, it wasn't him. "I'll go see."

"No!" She squawked the word, causing people nearby to look in their direction. Even someone who didn't know her wouldn't be able to mistake her panic.

"I'll take Mr. Potts with me." He gestured toward the leader of his security detail and, after rising, obstructed her view of the man until she looked up at him.

She'd said she hated it when he distracted her from her fears, but it was the only way he knew how to divert her when she got overwhelmed. But it also helped him.

He tilted her chin up and brushed his lips over hers, increasing the strength of his kiss until she kissed him back, even just briefly. "I'll just double-check, okay? You stay here. If it's him, I'll handle it. I promise."

It wasn't him, but he needed her to calm down. Talking about the man who'd tormented and blackmailed her had just made this fear materialize with the first person who looked passingly similar from a distance. Once he'd made sure she'd feel better.

He just wouldn't tell her he hadn't seen Ratliffe's photo yet.

By the end of the weekend, Quinn had come to understand the depth of Anais's fear over the photos and how the specter of Wayne haunted her.

Their outing in the park had generated the photos and videos online he'd hoped for, but his quiet, but admittedly strange, conversation with the man she'd mistaken for Ratliffe overshadowed their success. He'd been cordial and, despite his confusion, had produced identification when requested. He'd even been polite when Quinn had brought him to Anais for introductions, and through the embarrassment that had brought color back to her cheeks and sent her apologizing profusely—something she hadn't yet done with *him*.

At the charity brunch they'd attended late the following morning, he hadn't even needed to question the server she'd also mistakenly thought was Ratliffe. By then, he'd seen the man's file and had his mugshot on his phone to show her quietly, without causing a scene.

The most important thing for him to do with regard to their relationship had been to sort this situation out before anything else.

So now, nearing midnight on Tuesday evening, he knocked on Anais's door.

"What happened?" she whispered the second she opened the door, one hand shooting out to grab his arm and drag him inside before locking up.

She'd been asleep when he'd called to tell her he was coming, and her hair was delightfully messed up, but the pink silky gown and robe she wore took the majority of his attention. The low light in the room only accentuated the way the silk draped from her breasts and skimmed her waist. God, she looked good in it. He'd had a mission…

"I wanted to tell you tonight, as soon as it was done."

"So, tell me." She kept her voice low, pulled the short silky robe tighter around her, and went to perch on the sofa. "Stop dragging it out. Did something happen?"

He followed the conversation better once she stopped moving around and stopped jiggling. "I got the…"

The word *video* almost flew, but he checked himself in time. She'd never once mentioned a video to him—just pictures—and they scared her beyond reason alone. If she found out there was actual footage…

"You got the pictures?" she filled in, still speaking in low, but now frenzied tones.

"Yes." He cleared his throat. "And he's gone."

"What do you mean, he's gone?" She kept her voice low. "Is he dead?"

He finally found the wherewithal to look the room over and make sure his mother-in-law wasn't downstairs with them, and her question solidified. *Dead?*

"For God's sake, I didn't kill him."

The sudden exasperation in Quinn's voice had Anais flipping on the table lamp to better see him.

Lines she'd never noticed creased between his brows, evidence of a great deal of recent scowling. He looked tired. Exhausted, really. She patted the sofa cushion beside her and looked up at him. "Sit with me. I'll stop interrupting so you can tell me."

He more fell into the sofa than sat and, as soon as he'd settled, reached for her and tugged until she rested against his side. "I arranged early release from his grand larceny sentence; he was escorted with guards to the palace for a long talk, and made a deal that ended with me having the blackmail material, him without access to retrieve any copies and then out of the country with a tidy sum of money."

Before his words had a chance to settle, he'd upped the ante by dragging her into his lap.

Intimate and gentle despite his haggard appearance, he wrapped one arm around her waist and rested the other hand on her bare knee, thumb stroking in a leisurely way.

Distracting.

He sounded so certain that Wayne was out of their lives—that it was over. "What…?"

"I've spent the whole day with a loathsome man for you; do I not deserve a little bit of cuddling?"

The cheeky tone and lopsided grin were impossible not to return, and Anais felt herself smiling despite the subject of only seconds before. She propped her elbow on his shoulder and let her fingers scratch through the short, thick curling hair atop his head. "Is that how it works?"

He tilted his head into her hand and closed his eyes, but his hand stroked up her thigh and back, leaving those happy tingles racing over her skin. But his certainty was convincing, especially when it became clear how much he'd actually done.

"I don't know what to say," she whispered, feeling relief so palpable that this whole endeavor suddenly seemed possible. Or at least less terrifying. "You look tired."

"Long day," he confirmed, and opened his eyes, his hand still stroking up and down her thigh. He wanted to stay.

More. She wanted it too. "You could sleep here."

It took a lot to make the offer, so when he removed her hand from his hair and sketched a rueful smile she'd already started bracing herself for rejection.

"The sofa looks comfortable, but I'd rather a bed."

Since they'd met again, there had been kisses of all description—angry, overwhelming, gentle, sweet, tender—and all initiated by him. But she wanted to kiss him, even if it might not convince him she meant him to stay for more than sleep. She wanted her mouth tender from the day's growth of scratchy beard; she wanted that delicious burn all over her. She wanted to finally see the man's body that time and service had given him. He'd somehow managed to stay dressed that time in her office.

He hadn't stopped touching her, so she followed the will of her pounding heart and brushed her lips lightly against his. "I meant upstairs."

The way his fingers curled into her thigh and the uptick in his breathing said he wanted that too, but, as she tilted her head to deepen the kiss, he pulled back, regret in his eyes. "Is this gratitude?"

"Grat—?" She stopped and shook her head, leaning back to look at him. "No. It's not gratitude."

"Did you finally accept that I love you?" he asked, then flopped his head back, eyes closing. "Please say that's it, because I want to stay."

He couldn't be happy with progress; he wanted everything when he wanted it.

She didn't want to talk about this, not right now. "I know you care, but why does this have to be about love? It wasn't about love in my office. That was hate sex."

"That wasn't hate sex." He lifted his head sharply, instantly annoyed, but his hands stayed gentle, as if he'd willed them to be so, even while putting her off his lap.

His reaction shocked her almost as much as the grief she felt at losing the cage of his arms and the solid heat beneath her. But when he scooted an entire cushion away, that shock turned into grief. "What else would you call it?"

"Years of agony."

His bitter, disbelieving laugh robbed her of anything else to say. It took everything to keep the burning in her eyes from pouring salty rivers.

"What's it going to take? Do you think I half-violated a citizen's rights and kicked him out of the country because I just kind of like you and really like what's between your legs?"

Still no words came, even when he rose and stomped for the door.

"So that you can't be further confused, I'll make it clear. When you accept why I'm doing all this, I'll go upstairs with you. That's it."

Love. She knew what he meant.

If she said what he wanted to hear, it would just be because she wanted him to stay and stop looking at her like that.

Even if it was exactly how he should look at her—shock and bitterness that meant he was reconsidering this foolish idea.

"Did you look at the photos?"

"That's what you want to know?" He shook his head, jaw gritted as he closed his eyes for long, stuttering heartbeats. "I saw enough to confirm it was you. That's it."

Which should've made her feel a little better, but didn't. "Where are they?"

"Penthouse safe. You can have them after the wedding." The smile he gave her was all teeth, sharp and unhappy. "Think of it as the world's most messed-up wedding gift."

"More blackmail to marry you? Is *that* an act of love?"

"Collateral," he corrected. "If you love someone, set them free? I'm supposed to just let you go? Because you said you wanted me to fight for you. You can't have it both ways."

CHAPTER EIGHT

ANAIS WALKED THE LONG, winding corridors of Sisters of Grace Hospital, her hand tucked into Quinn's. From the dampness of his palm, she knew he was worried. Not that anyone else could see it—the military bearing seemed marrow-deep now, to the point that he practically marched and she had to jog to keep up.

Ben's surgery started in an hour, having been scheduled with remarkable speed during the few days she'd been away from Almsford—something Quinn finessed.

"He'll be all right," she whispered to him, but he gave no sign he'd heard her until the door to their private waiting room finally swung shut behind them.

It had barely clicked closed before he tugged her into his arms and seemed to deflate a little until his chin rested on her shoulder.

She said it again, no matter how close it felt to the kind of assurances she'd been trained to never give. For him she'd forget that training. "It's going to work. He'll do great."

He released her and pushed a white handled shopping bag into her hands—the one she'd thought carried a gift for his friend. "I asked if, as one of Ben's doctors, you could pop in and out of the surgery to keep us updated on how everything was going. Would you?"

Ben was still pre-op, with a long surgery ahead, and Quinn was already a breath away from completely wrecked.

A peek into the bag confirmed her suspicions: scrubs.

Aside from demanding she marry him, Quinn had asked very little from her so far; really nothing compared to all she'd asked of him. Wear this gorgeous ring, go for a walk and picnic in the park, attend tonight's Independence Day party at the American Embassy… All requests made in service to his Make People Like Anais campaign. This was the first thing he'd asked for himself.

As awkward as it was to barge into another surgeon's OR, she didn't want to say no. She remembered clinging to her computer for any news she could scavenge in the days after Quinn had been injured.

Waiting when the life of someone you loved hung by a thread was absolute torture.

"If they'll allow it," she ventured. "I don't have privileges at this hospital."

"I cleared it all. Thank you." He breathed out slowly, a small amount of tension ebbing from his worried brow. "Rosalie's in with him right now, but she's going to be in here with us, waiting. I'm sure she'll appreciate updates too."

"I'll do whatever I can. Is there somewhere I can change?" She'd thrown herself—quite unsuccessfully—at the man only days ago. It'd be pointless to get weird about changing her clothes in front of him now. "Or can you stand against the door? I'll be quick."

His brows popped up, but he nodded and went to plant his shoulder against the only exit. "Want me to turn around?"

Just a polite question; the man already looked like he had no intention of moving, the confidence she'd been missing immediately returned.

"You've seen it all. Your body's the mystery here."

"How's my body a mystery?" Quinn asked, his eyes tracking each button's release down her front.

The weight of his gaze on her, changing in a hospital waiting room, shouldn't have brought back that maddening tingle—a feeling she was starting to make peace with and maybe even enjoy a little. Aside from him touching her, it was the next best thing. Even when it started feeling more like a striptease than a simple matter of necessity.

Her blouse fell open, and Anais had never been so happy to have selected a pretty white lace panty set over her usual combination of whatever she'd blindly grabbed from the underwear drawer. The pressure of looming princesshood made her feel the need to dress in her best, and that even included the bits no one would see unless she was in a tragic accident. Under Quinn's plan, she now felt obligated to wear pretty, matching underwear.

"Your body's different." She tried to sound unaffected, but she might've turned so that her underthings were displayed anyway. *He'd* turned her down, after all. By his heavy-lidded stare, he was at least distracted. "I bet you're at least thirty-five pounds heavier than when I last saw you undressed."

He'd not undressed for the office sex that Quinn's vehemence troubled her ability to categorize. She'd been the only one naked for that.

She shimmied out of the baby-blue pencil skirt and retrieved the scrubs.

"Your body is different too," he said thickly. Then, with way more energy, he added, "You got a tattoo!"

Before she could say anything about it, her door guard left his post and crossed to her.

"Quinn!" she squawked, grabbed the scrubs top and darted around him to block the door herself. "You are supposed to be blocking the door with your extra pounds!"

"Hold still. Infinity symbol… Tiny writing." He fell to one knee, grabbed her by the hips and spun her around to get a better look at the slender ribbon of script circling back on itself. *"Today's courage is tomorrow's peace."*

The words had his brows pinching and he looked up at her, working on the meaning in relation to her.

"I know what you're thinking." She tugged the top on and carefully stepped around him. "Stay at the door this time. I need the bottoms."

"That's not what I was thinking."

"No. You're thinking, with a motto like that I should've handled Wayne on my own."

"Wrong again."

Of course she was. People didn't get tattoos to remind them of things they'd like to forget. She'd made the mark on her flesh in the hopes of getting it off her heart.

*Leave today, have peace tomorrow...*only it hadn't happened that quickly. But she didn't want to talk about it right then. "Okay, maybe I don't know then."

She tugged on the bottoms and, after her usually nimble fingers refused to tie the drawstring, gave up and just stuffed her utterly impractical and improper kitten-heeled feet into the shoe covers from the bottom of the bag.

He was still watching her; she could feel it, vibrating the air, bringing on another round of tingles and an accelerated heartbeat that could either be desire or the sick feeling this conversation summoned.

Let it drop. Today was already too emotionally fraught for him to engage in this.

"Do you want to know?" He obviously didn't feel the desire to let go, but the low rumble his voice developed echoed other desires.

Ignore those other desires too; he'd made clear the price and she wasn't willing to pay. "Will it bring me peace tomorrow?"

The laugh she got in return eased her a little, another form of distraction.

"You're kind of hit and miss on the application of this motto."

"I'm a work in progress. It's there to remind me."

"That change takes courage and an act of will?"

She nodded, her throat suddenly unwilling to let sound through.

Please, stop there.

"Did it work with me?"

When he said those things, it always made her feel as if the ground were falling away from under her.

It would do her no good to deflect again; that his question knocked the air out of her answered well enough. "I don't know how to answer that."

"Truth is always appreciated."

Not true. He wouldn't want her if he knew the truth about her lackluster judgment, morals…the battered self-esteem she fought against all the time. "In a way, it did. In other ways, it didn't."

He nodded in a slow, measuring way. "How did it make things…not better?"

"You know how," she said, but couldn't find any strength to make her words more than a ghost of the feeling she'd wallowed in for years after leaving.

"Tell me anyway." He was near her now, near enough to touch, near enough his whispered command felt like a warm request.

"I missed you." Because she'd already admitted she'd left for his good once, not because she'd wanted to. "But I stopped being so afraid all the time. If you're angry about that, I get it—I sacrificed *us* to save *me*. And you. Your family. It was the only thing I could do."

"And now?"

He wanted her admission—and Anais could only pretend to herself that she didn't love him when he wasn't with her—but she didn't want to accept that he still loved her. Or had ever loved her. It meant taking all the blame for their marital failure; it meant saying his emotional distance would've made no difference. That was something she wasn't even able to consider.

If only she'd known how to make him listen back then.

If only she'd tried harder.

If only she'd been stronger for them both.

The limousine stopped outside the American embassy in the heart of the capital, Anais and Quinn in the back. A red, white and blue awning, patriotic sashes, flowers and decorations lent color to the gray stone nineteenth-century building, honoring the country's Independence Day celebrations.

Anais smoothed her hands over the sleek up-do Aunt Helen had wrestled her frequently frizzy waves into. Still intact. A quick inventory of her sapphire dress reassured her further. Unrumpled, at least from the front.

"You look gorgeous," Quinn said beside her, capturing one of her fussing hands along with her attention, but making no move to exit the car yet. "Did you know they do this at almost all their embassies? Even the American Embassy in London."

"I wondered," she admitted, going with his efforts to distract her, even if he'd not really picked a subject that could do anything to take her attention from the knot in her middle or a curiously jelly-like weakness in her arms she'd bet would worsen when she had to teeter her way up the red-carpeted entrance where all the cameras could legitimately film them tonight without violating Quinn's request for space.

Quinn's car door swung open, a smartly suited young man holding it for them, but Quinn leaned closer to her, a soft chuckle announcing the joking tone that had always delighted her but which she'd only heard a handful of times since coming home. "I always wondered if it was considered rude. It seems kind of rude."

Good mood undamped since Ben's successful surgery hours earlier. She shared his relief and happiness for his best friend—and, having watched him with Ben's fiancée the whole day, fully understood what the couple meant to

Quinn, which invested her even more in their now hope-filled future.

But the prospect of an official diplomatic function in formal attire? Yeah, that put a damper on her glee.

She made herself come up with words; talking about anything was better than silently worrying about how she'd perform tonight.

"I don't know. I guess I never thought about it. I wasn't even aware they celebrated it here. Growing up, anytime I saw random fireworks displays in the city, I'd watch, wonder briefly what they were about, then go back to whatever I was doing—reading, most likely." At home, the salon or the library—the extents of her teenage territory.

Her knees wobbled as he led her up the carpet, but the long gown hid that manifestation of fear turning her bones to cartilage.

Quinn didn't miss it. He closed his free hand over hers and continued in low, conspiratorial murmurings as flashes went off on either side of them, which she'd darned well smile for over the butterfly tornados in her belly. "Like going to your ex's house to throw a *Remember-When-I-Threw-All-Your-Things-On-The-Lawn* party."

She smiled for real, despite her nervousness. "Actually, it's considered American soil. Not sure about the skies above, but this ground is theirs. So, welcome to the USA on Independence Day."

It made her feel a little better, talking with him, or maybe just doing anything with him that could distract her from the worry that had knotted her up in one form or another all day.

And maybe it also helped to get to be a wee smarty-pants. Quinn had always appreciated that about her—she got to be something besides a jabbering idiot once tonight before she did something stupid and laughter chased her from the party.

"Been studying?"

"Yes. And it's probably against some custom, making fun of a nation's favorite holiday. Although, having been to a number of Fourth of July celebrations in the States, some sort of ruckus wouldn't be out of line, though my previous experiences might clash with tonight's festivities."

"Which would be…?"

"A barbecue, copious amounts of beer, ill-advised and inebriated handling of barely regulated explosives, a possible trip to the Emergency Department, and prayers for a nearby fire extinguisher."

"Definitely at odds with a black-tie dress code."

They breezed through a decorated lobby with security checking invitations. Open double doors led into a wide, expansive room probably only for entertaining, and which made her double down on her nerves.

Quinn steered her towards official-looking people and made greetings and introductions. She had to release his arm to shake hands or risk looking even more like the lot of them terrified her, but regretted it immediately. His hand had steadied her a little; without it her smile trembled in a way that couldn't be missed.

By the time she'd gotten through her third set of introductions, Quinn steered her to a corner and turned her to face him.

Standing so close, when she met his gaze, the gathering party faded a little behind him. When he cupped her cheeks and planted a sweet, chaste kiss on her lips, the din faded even more in a wash of warmth and a strange peace. Their first kiss since the fight.

"Do I have your attention now?" The teasing note in his voice softened the criticism she always felt too vulnerable to in this kind of situation. "You have to stop fidgeting."

Her grimace couldn't be thwarted.

"Everyone's looking at me," she tried to explain, and immediately heard how ridiculous it sounded. Right behind that, she actually processed his words and felt herself twisting the engagement ring around her finger. "I didn't realize I was fidgeting."

His thumbs began stroking lightly over her cheeks and he kissed her again, this time well enough to send shivers to her belly and the tingles she'd developed a begrudging love of to the rest of her. This was what she'd always found so addictive about the man; he could pour molten desire into her by simply touching her face. A few seconds of kissing sky-rocketed the effect.

When her heart pounded enough to jiggle her chest, he lifted his head again. The playful spark had vanished, and now his heavily lidded eyes told her he was regretting that sexual détente he'd issued.

"People are looking at you because you're beautiful and elegant. And because we're news—more than usual because we asked not to be news. They're not watching because you're messing up."

"Except fidgeting and having attention issues."

His response was a gentle smile, then a brief brush of his lips on her forehead. "We don't have long before they call us to dinner. I rang ahead to confirm we'd be seated together. Relax. Be yourself. What do you think they see when they look at you that's so objectionable?"

"I don't know."

His raised brows bid her try again; he wasn't going to let her blow the question off. Releasing her cheeks, he took her hands and waited.

"They see uncultured riff-raff. Or a devious, low-born she-wolf who tricked you into marriage—"

"No. I didn't ask what they *said* about you," Quinn interrupted, "or do you *believe* you tricked me into marriage with your magic vagina?"

The words *magic vagina* were like a tiny hammer to her knee, and her foot sprang forward before she could think it through. Her toes bounced off his shin hard enough for him to wince, but it conveyed how seriously she'd always taken that particular slight...

"I think they'll see me kick someone important," she

grunted. "Or make some other mistake in protocol or manners. It doesn't matter that yesterday I downloaded instructions for American diplomats on how to behave at social functions. I read it three times, but I might miss something small, or do something dumb and…"

"They'll think you're an idiot?"

She felt heat rush into her face and she forced herself to nod. "My intelligence is the only acceptable thing about me. Even when the country was at the height of their hatred and disapproval, that was the one back-handed compliment I got. *How could someone so intelligent think an illegitimate commoner eloping with a prince could ever be acceptable?*"

He leaned in again as if to kiss her and she pulled back.

"If I mess up or do something stupid I'm nothing special at all." The words came in a rush, but heated up a little at the end as she whisper-hissed, "I don't even have a magic vagina."

"Oh, yes, you do." He laughed at that. "But, more importantly, one mistake doesn't make anyone into an irredeemable idiot."

"We have this thing called the Internet—and yes, it does. Mistakes live forever online. Ask celebrities with their awkward school pictures everywhere."

He looked briefly pained and out of his depth, but a slow breath and a shake of his head released it. "I'm not going to talk you out of this tonight. But you just smiled a little. Why did you smile?"

She'd smiled? A quick inventory of her face confirmed it. Her cheeks did feel recently bunched. "I'm not sure. I guess somewhere in that I stopped feeling so afraid. Maybe even felt a little good?" No wonder he liked to use distraction on her. "Or maybe I felt better because I kicked you."

"Do you want to kick me again? I'm here to be supportive."

The offer made her cheeks start to bunch again, so she leaned up to give him the kiss she'd dodged.

"Or that. Kicks, kisses, groping behind Old Glory over there, I'm good for all of that. In the name of being a supportive husband."

"Okay, enough with the husband business, support man," she said but didn't step away from him.

"Enough with the husband business *for now*," he agreed, then jerked his head toward the party. "You ready to go back in?"

And...smile gone. She forced a fake one that was at least steadier now.

"Follow my lead and remember they're our allies; this isn't some tense diplomatic situation. You lived there for years; you *have* things to talk about."

She wouldn't turn down a little pep-talk. The talking was what helped.

"I do think you should reconsider your position on alcohol. It helps sometimes."

That she would turn down.

They returned to circulating and she took every spare second he was in conversation to examine others in attendance and mentally compare herself before switching up her posture to mimic the most graceful she noticed.

By the time dinner had been rung, she'd nearly gotten control of her worrying. No matter what Quinn thought about her alcohol prohibition, she had hard evidence and personal experience on how stupid she could be when her self-esteem and inadequacies collided with booze. She might end up topless, giving the ambassador a lap dance. And the ambassador was a long-married grandmother.

As soon as they sat, Quinn snagged her closest hand and kept hold of her between courses—sometimes beneath the table, sometimes on top. Even when he'd half turned away from her to engage in conversation with his neighbors.

It helped, but her table neighbors' social graces made up the difference, not hers. They drew her into conversation so subtly she didn't even realize the subject had turned to her until she'd answered several questions.

How was it to be home?

What State had she lived in?

Was she excited about the wedding?

These were easy to answer, mostly. The wedding talk? At least she knew what she was expected to say and fell into that narrative well enough.

"How did you choose your specialty?"

The steak she'd been enjoying seemed to transform, from charred delight to a ten-ton boulder in her belly.

The woman who'd asked probably thought it a completely innocent question, but easy answers came to an end and she had to put her fork and knife down before she dropped them.

She could give the standard response she'd used—a patient during her rotations had captured her heart. It was touching, and complete fiction.

The truth would maintain Quinn's narrative, but…

Quinn taking her hand beneath the table again made her aware of how long she'd taken to start answering. She glanced his way to find him watching her, interested brows up, no censure there.

She wasn't sure whether to say it, or even *how* to say it. How she should even feel? Would someone secure in her relationship feel that old pain, or the shame the admission would still trigger? Would a normal person have gotten past it all? Would she own it, flaws and all? Would she feel the aching sense of exposure Anais still had to swallow past?

She didn't know where the decision came from, only that Quinn's hand in hers gave her the strength to say it.

With a steadying breath, she started to speak.

"I was a first-year general surgery fellow when I changed to orthopedics. When Quinn was injured." She stopped. Having never heard him speak of his injury in public added another layer of hesitation. Would he mind? Truth, he'd claimed, was always appreciated. A quick glance showed no dismay, just sharpening interest.

"Like everyone else, I'd heard he'd been shot, but not where, or how seriously for a couple of very long days."

The hand holding hers lifted their joined hands back to the table top; she took the silent encouragement.

As soon as she'd heard he was all right, she'd walled those toxic feelings off—spent no time thinking of the days and the hurt she'd buried behind them. Those days had been so packed with terror, guilt, and worry worse even than when she'd left him. Self-preservation demanded zero reflection. So there was no practiced, logical story to tell, just a rush of words and emotions, unfiltered, unordered, far too revealing.

"By the time his injury and amputation were announced, I was a mess. Happy he was alive, so relieved that I felt guilty over effectively being happy he'd lost his fingers." Her throat thickened. She reached for her water. Over her glass, she saw the number of eyes focused on her, heard the silence that had fallen, and felt the scorching tears gathering.

It was too much. She was saying too much. Every part of her wanted to make an excuse, to flee the table. Except the hand tucked into his, and the part of her that wanted him to know that, although she'd left, she'd still been with him in her heart through those dark, dreadful days.

But she couldn't look at him.

"I changed my track the day I heard. I guess I wanted to help people who were going through the same thing he was going through."

His quickened breathing told her he'd been affected, as did the slight tremble of his wine glass she saw in her peripheral vision.

Was that enough? She lowered her head to dab at her eyes, praying for the topic to shift.

"You wanted to help him, but you couldn't," the woman

summarized for her, and Anais could only nod, mouth twisting to control her trembling lower lip.

Quinn lifted her hand. The brush of his lips across her knuckles pulled her watery gaze sideways to him. If she looked at him fully, she'd lose her mind and control of the unpredictable sobbing that had carried her through those days.

CHAPTER NINE

WAIT STAFF CIRCLED the table, placing dessert plates before each guest—something fruity in red, white and blue. Quinn couldn't focus on it. If he could harness the current coming through Anais's hand now *gripping* his, he could power the capital.

He turned more to face her, pretending it was to share a dessert with her when really every ounce of his willpower was engaged in fighting his instinct to spirit her away. Just to hold her. Just to put his arms around her and rock through the pain he still felt vibrating through her.

He felt the weight of everyone's gaze now—everyone but her—but he couldn't blame them. Or her. But he needed to look at her as desperately as her grip said she needed to keep hold of him.

Mechanically, she went about a few bites of the berry concoction. She ate, but didn't taste it; her half-bowed head and blank eyes made it clear.

Before they'd made a dent in the dessert the fireworks display was announced, and guests departed the table for the veranda to the rear gardens. She started too, but Quinn tugged her close enough to wrap an arm around her waist and steer her to the dance floor instead. His obligation to remain through the fireworks display was the only thing keeping him from taking her away with him.

The lights in the great room fell, to minimize the distraction through the wide veranda windows separating them from the guests outside watching the sky, but the dark also made it feel secluded, almost private.

"We're not going out?" she whispered, but turned into his arms as he steered her around the floor.

"I can see from here," he said, not wanting to break the spell between them and what it told him.

She loved him. She'd never stopped loving him. But it felt as if a stiff breeze could blow her away, so he folded her into his arms and rested his cheek against her temple.

Tilting her head, she whispered by his ear, "Are you okay?"

Worried about him. More proof.

"A little overwhelmed," he admitted, unable to summon a better answer, unable to make a clever or cajoling response, the words aching in his chest. "I didn't know that about your specialty. I'd wondered, but I should've asked. I should've sat down with you and just talked, not about all this...just to know. What I missed. We should've found time to sit down."

He felt her nodding, felt her pull him a little tighter, even felt the regret rolling off her.

"We've never really done much of that. Only when we were dating."

The softly spoken words burned. He tried to think about times after they'd eloped when they'd just sat and talked about anything for longer than a few minutes, but he couldn't. In that moment, swallowing past the lump in his throat, he was glad for the dark, even glad for the way his lungs refused to draw a complete breath—it drove home the part he'd played in the downfall of their marriage—she hadn't ducked out of conversations he'd started, not once.

"We'll do better this time."

Her nod expressed her hesitation as much as it could be agreement.

Yes, she still loved him, but that hadn't stopped her from leaving the first time. He had to do better.

"I think you could've talked to me about Ratliffe if we'd had that kind of marriage. A relationship you felt safe in."

"Maybe." Her hand slid to the back of his neck and she kneaded as she gave him that single word.

No matter how long ago it had been, she was still raw. He felt it too, but that same wound had started to heal in him the day he'd found her again, when it started to feel like something he could control.

"We've got a good forty-five minutes right now." He kissed the side of her neck just as the first flash of sparkling light illuminated the dark room and the music erupted with the loud, alarming bang.

"Quinn?" She leaned back and the fireworks illuminated her face; eyes wide with concern broke through the wariness that had grabbed him.

"I'm fine," he said quickly, then forced himself to relax. "Just startled me."

"I didn't think about the fireworks. Are you sure? We can go. I can..." She paused, her eyes swiveled toward the ceiling as she tried to scheme. "I could faint or something as a cover?"

Her comical attempt at subterfuge relaxed him further. "I'm really all right. I don't have PTSD. Just a bit of...inattention to anything that isn't you right now."

Even in the green glow of the skies, he saw her blush. Then he saw her focus on his mouth with a kind of intention that might as well be invitation. Quinn took it, pulling her closer again and brushing his lips over hers. The lingering strawberry from dessert only magnified her natural sweetness, and the sweet ache that had been growing in his chest since her story.

She'd given them an out and he could happily sink into her kisses, into the soft sighs she rewarded him with as he deepened the exploration of her mouth. When she stroked her tongue past his lips, he tumbled into the mind-blanking bliss that always came when touching her—but this time it came with a little needle of loss.

They'd been talking. He wanted to talk to her right now more than he wanted to kiss her, even if only just.

The music accompanying the thundering explosions shifted into loud, enthusiastic twentieth-century rock'n'roll, and he went with it—sealing the deep, toe-curling kisses with a slow, tender one.

She smiled even before her eyes opened back up and, with it, the heaviness that had crept over them lifted.

They were still on the dance floor, and he actually felt like dancing.

He started her swaying, in the way of two people who couldn't let go of one another and couldn't spare enough attention to pick their feet off the floor. "Tell me about medical school."

"That'll take much longer than forty-five minutes, unless you narrow it down."

"Good point." He squeezed her again and reformulated the first question. Then, as soon as she'd given a brief answer, he asked another, shooting forward another and another, gathering facts and amusing her by making her slow dance sway through "God Bless America" and "Born in the USA"…

The fireworks display passed in a heartbeat, long before Quinn was done asking questions, the lights inside had come back up and guests once more invaded the alone time he'd had with his wife.

Faster than could've ever been considered diplomatically acceptable, Quinn had whisked Anais to the US Ambassador and made their farewells to a knowing smile blessedly free of rancor for the representative of their host nation who'd failed entirely in all things diplomatic since dessert.

In the limo on the way to her house, their conversation turned to him. Even though the greed he felt to know more

about her railed against it, he fought the desire to redirect—
she needed to understand him if she would ever trust him
enough to stay.

They talked about his adventures with Ben, things she'd
heard about him via the media through the years, she even
had him telling her a childhood story she'd heard before but
which still made her laugh.

"I feel a bit silly offering tea in my living room while
we're both in formalwear," she said, locking her front door
behind them. She hadn't asked whether he intended to stay
the night, and he was glad for it. If he had to make the call
right now, he'd say he was staying, and that would force
a different conversation. Knowing she still loved him, he
could wait for other admissions.

She kicked off her shoes, getting comfortable.

"If it helps, I'd be happy to strip down to my skivvies
and drink tea. So long as Sharon won't come downstairs
and be horrified to find me in my boxers."

One corner of her mouth lifted in tandem with her hand,
a half-shrug and a half-grin to his silly offer. "Mom's gone
to Aunt Helen's for the night to play cards. If she'd been
here alone all evening waiting for me, she'd just have worried herself sick. Her heart tends to go out of rhythm when
her blood pressure rises."

She'd mentioned her mother's illness a few times, but
he'd never asked for specifics. That seemed like something
else he should remedy.

"Is it bad?" He took her hand, even though knowing
would make it harder to force Anais's hand with the wedding—a threat that already felt inconceivable to carry out.

"It could be much worse than it is," she said, stepping a
little closer so that their arms weren't stretched to the limit
across the space between them, still happy to touch him,
something he felt pathetically grateful for. "I'm hopeful that
by the time surgery becomes imperative, the procedure will
be safer. It's pretty safe now, but there's one sneaky, deadly,

irreversible complication that hits about one percent of patients, and by the time it's detected it's almost always too late. As long as the condition is livable with medication and lifestyle management, I don't want her to risk it."

He could understand that. He'd take that situation with his grandfather in a heartbeat, but getting the old man to come around to the same way of thinking hadn't yet worked for him. "Sneaky, deadly, irreversible…words you never want associated with a heart procedure."

"No."

He stepped closer so that she tilted her head back to look up at him. "I didn't mean to turn the conversation to sad subjects, but I guess we do need to learn how to discuss painful topics too."

She nodded, but the frown that crept over her face let him know the instant her thoughts drifted to some other painful subject, and hung there.

"A kiss for your thoughts," he prodded.

"Not money?"

"Are you kidding? My kisses are far more valuable than money." To prove it, he dropped his lips to her mouth—fleeting affection. "Play along. I've got a fragile ego."

"Not unless you're collecting other people's egos as pets," she snorted and then reached for his other hand—the one that she always insisted on holding, even when he tried to maneuver her to his right. Still she didn't give voice to what was on her mind, just stroked his hand for a moment then, just as quickly, dropped it, freeing hers to slide under his lapels and over his shoulders, easing the jacket down his arms and off.

Waiting for her to talk was horrible. Especially when, in exchange, he had small delicate hands on his chest, burning through the thin barriers of his clothing. Focus diminishing…

"The suspense is killing me. I gave you the kiss; you're supposed to pay up with words now."

"I'm helping you get comfortable," she argued, folding the jacket over one of her arms then reaching for the ridiculous American flag bow tie he'd gotten only for the flamboyant party.

"I can't multi-task. I'm either all in this conversation or I'm going to want to enjoy being undressed. That's it."

"Okay," she said slowly. "I've been avoiding asking you about your tours. I don't know if you need to talk about them, or if you want to, or if talking would do anything good for either of us."

Good for either of us. That part was what stuck out to him. She was a little afraid to ask, but felt compelled nevertheless.

"I can talk about my tours in a far more civilized manner than when I told you about my hand." Recalling that conversation put tonight's revelation in an even harsher light. Guilt bit even through the feel of her gentle touches, and lingered as she hung the jacket in the coat closet.

He wouldn't apologize for it again; that would turn the conversation, make it harder for her.

"Ask, love. Ask me anything."

She closed the door and leaned against it, compelling him to come to her when she didn't return. He could control his need to touch her, but not if she felt far away, if he couldn't feel her heat and wrap himself in her scent.

"Why didn't you come home after you were wounded? I know it was offered, automatic, expected even. You had to fight to remain." She'd been serving wounded soldiers long enough to have wondered, but he didn't even have to ask to know she'd had that question in her heart for years.

It was right there in her furrowed brows—old pain, worry she'd sunk into years ago, something he couldn't even blame her for anymore.

He couldn't blame her, and he didn't want her to blame herself. She would if he answered.

After he'd decided to return to active duty, he'd allowed

himself to fantasize that she was worrying about him. Pretended she was suffering over him. Even sometimes in the hospital during his recovery, when he recalled the deaths of so many friends and how easily it could've been him, he'd pictured her mourning him if it had. All immature ways to handle his grief over losing her, but it had all come from a deep-seated belief that she'd never feel those things, even if the worst had come to pass.

Knowing it would've been all he'd imagined and more made it even harder to say the words.

"Ask anything except that?" she ventured when he failed to find words.

"I don't want us to stop talking."

"It's a conversation-stopper?"

"Feels like it."

The worry was still in her eyes, but she kept on. "We need to learn to discuss painful subjects."

His words from only moments before jostled his conscience, despite her not giving them even a hint of mockery.

"It's not that I don't want it to hurt *me*." It was the only way he knew to put it.

Her slow nod and pained expression hit him harder than her silence.

Continue or not? He couldn't always trust his instincts when it came to Anais.

"I'm going to put the kettle on and change. You think about a way to say it," she directed then just left the room, as if words were so easy. She knew better.

Though, to be fair, he was probably the one hiding the most right now. She still thought Ratliffe had just taken photos of her—she didn't have any idea about the video. But this conversation wasn't that one. Focus on one trauma at a time.

Quinn undid the top few buttons of his shirt, then rolled up his sleeves to the elbow and sat on the sofa, but he couldn't make himself comfortable. If they'd sorted out their relationship already, he'd rip off the formalwear and get comfortable. Hell, he'd rip off all the formalwear, carry her upstairs and kiss every inch of her—especially the inches that made her writhe and moan.

Where they stood now, stripping down for comfort would be even weirder than late night tea in a tuxedo in her living room.

And thinking about how uncomfortable he felt was kind of a dodge for thinking about the subject that made him even more uncomfortable.

He puffed a breath and laid his head back on the sofa cushions.

There was no gentle, non-accusatory way to put it, which meant it could only end one of two ways: by starting a fight with her, or with her just taking more blame onto herself.

She wafted back down the stairs in pajamas that looked equal parts comfortable and silly—littered with hearts and, inexplicably, cartoon monkeys. Somehow the baggy tee and shorts made his modified formalwear look like the most ridiculous outfit in the room.

It was a quick trip to the kitchen and she returned with two steaming mugs and a package of cookies tucked under one arm, but he was still unprepared for the subject.

"Come up with the right words?" she asked, placing the lot on the table and sitting beside him crossways, giving him no gentle lead-in.

"No."

"Then just say it. However it comes out, that's how you need to say it. I didn't have the luxury of rehearsing a painful subject at dinner. It didn't shut down conversation, but seems to have started it."

Just say something.

He couldn't stop his hands scrubbing over his face. He hated feeling helpless. "I went back because I thought I'd be going to a new unit with Ben."

"You didn't think he'd want you to be safe, away from the fighting?"

"I knew he would've, but I wasn't so wounded as to be incapable of service. Leaving would've been selfish."

Dangerous word...

He stared at the ceiling but there weren't any answers there, just an expanse of white. And a tiny spider, which he could probably point out and distract her from this conversation...

"Why would that hurt me?" she asked, not raising her voice—still calm, but too perceptive to be dodged. "What aren't you saying?"

His head throbbed behind one eye and he mashed his palm against it.

Didn't help.

Touching her would help. He caught her closest hand again and worked his thick, clumsy-feeling fingers between her slender digits. Her thumb stroked his skin, helping more with that connective current still buzzing between them.

"Because it felt like I'd be abandoning them. Him. It wasn't some kind of respect for duty or the honor for service that got me back in a forward area. When my grandfather sent me into the military I had to make a new family, and I couldn't abandon them."

Like everyone here abandoned me.

He didn't need to say the words; he could already hear them echoing in her mind.

Her thumb stopped stroking and silence fell as she digested it. Even without looking at her, he felt her staring at his hand, and impulse confirmed it as he gave in to the need to see her.

But it was the distinct lack of yelling that spoke the loudest. She was taking it onto herself.

"It wasn't just you," he said softly. "It felt that way with my family too."

"Because of me."

"Because of *me*." He leaned on the word. "If it had just been a failed marriage, everything would've gone differently. Seven years of service has given me a different perspective. I know I was spoiled—I always thought of my wants first. I wanted you—I made it happen. Like everything else in my life. I don't begrudge them my military service—I came to love it pretty quickly. I would've easily been a lifer if I hadn't been called home."

She nodded at appropriate intervals, assuring him that she'd at least heard him, but when she slipped her hand free and roughly shoved the rolled cuff up to bare his left arm—specifically the scar peeking below the cuff at his elbow—he wondered if she'd heard him after all.

"You went through another attack?"

Redirects were better than wallowing in what he'd laid out.

"That happens in a war zone, but I'm going to assume you're asking if I was wounded in another attack. And, yes, I've picked up a few non-life-threatening wounds here and there."

"A few?" Her voice rose sharply and she climbed over to straddle his lap while her fingers tore through the buttons on his shirt, her face a picture of such horror he was almost afraid to say anything else.

"Non-lethal," he said slowly, but leaned forward as she shoved the shirt off his shoulders, then attacked the tee shirt beneath.

The word hadn't penetrated; she searched him as if he carried live explosives.

"No one reported other wounds. It wasn't in the news or in the papers. Mom would've told me if she'd heard anything like that, and I had alerts. I had alerts, Quinn. I had Internet alerts to tell me when anything happened with you. There wasn't anything reported!" She leaned back enough to look at his chest, and found both scars at once.

"I didn't report them. They were nothing…"

"Dammit, Quinton Corlow! What else?"

"Should I just list any wound I've had since I saw you? These are nothing."

"Was this another bullet?"

"No," he answered as her gentle fingers stroked over a puckered scar on his right flank. "That was a little piece of shrapnel. Again, it was nothing. It barely got past the body armor."

"And this?" She gingerly touched a three-inch slice of a scar on his other side.

"That was a bullet. Grazed me."

"Any other places hidden by your clothes?"

He tried not to look at the scar on his left arm, the one she'd initially spotted but had gotten so carried away in searching she seemed to have forgotten. He'd like her to keep forgetting it; he'd like her to forget anything to do with *that* injury. "Just what you've seen."

Nothing more to see. Move along...

"None of these required surgical intervention?" She caught his face and those gorgeous blue-green eyes drilled into him.

He wanted to be annoyed, but he had a seven-year void to fill where he would've killed for her attention and concern. "The bullet didn't lodge in me. The shrapnel was so shallow I grabbed it with tweezers. Only needed antibiotics and butterfly strips."

"And this one?" She let go of his cheek and reached for his left arm, his heart plummeting as she lifted it to examine the scar. "A fourth attack?"

"No."

"Two at once?"

He nodded and, for all his talk of openness and learning to discuss painful things, he let instinct take over—to protect her from further gory details as he protected family. She was family again. Gripping her hips, he tugged her forward until that hot little mound of flesh between her thighs ground into him.

Pressed against him, it wasn't even a stretch to trace kisses along the side of her neck, to nose into the strawberry locks she'd let down when she'd gone upstairs to change.

Anais's breath caught at the pressure of his rapidly responding body between her legs. The treacherously light brush of his lips along the tender, sensitive skin below her ear brought a melting heaviness that demanded more.

He'd survived—the living heat of him rocked beneath her, urging her fully against him, compelling her arms to slide around the wide breadth of his shoulders. He was safe now. It might feel urgent to know, but so did the desire to be closer.

His arms around her, his hands beneath her pants squeezing bare flesh as he ground her purposefully against him... made his intentions completely clear.

"Let's go upstairs," he murmured against her ear between kisses, and the words somehow brought their situation back into hazy focus.

He'd said *no* on Tuesday. Not without words from her.

Slowly, understanding began to seep back in.

They'd been talking and he'd suddenly shifted direction. She knew that pattern.

She pushed against his shoulders to open enough space to look at him.

"Why now? You've changed your mind about sleeping with me?"

The sigh that burst from him accompanied by those previously heavily lidded eyes snapping closed answered even before he flopped his head back against the cushioned seatback.

No words. No denial. No agreement.

He *was* distracting her.

"You ass!" She shoved herself off his lap hard and didn't stop until she was a good meter away.

"See? I knew this would lead to a fight."

"You tell me about that scar right now!" She ran back through the conversation. He thought knowing would hurt her. "That happened when your hand was shot? A second bullet?"

He hadn't lifted his head or opened his eyes. She'd have wondered if he'd fallen asleep if not for the vein pulsing wildly in his throat.

"No."

"Shrapnel?"

"Yes."

His flat answers made it worse—as if she was going to hear he'd been injured by friendly fire, or while hammering on a live bullet in some suicide attempt.

The ring...

"I thought you said it was stuck into your palm." She meant to shout. She meant to scream. But the words were just above a whisper.

Enough to hear her, he opened his eyes but there still was no life in his words. "Not the ring."

"No?"

He shook his head and a pleading look descended over him.

"Worse than the ring?"

What could be worse than the ring?

"Any additional information about that is going to make it worse. Just let it go."

"Please tell me."

"Bone."

One word dropped and her body went haywire, like every possible sensation fighting for control of the nerves in her skin. Cold. Burning. Tingling. Jolting pain. Her hands flew to cover her face, as if that could protect her from it.

The darkness behind her eyes filled with terrible visuals to accompany the words. A slow motion track of a bullet striking his hand, then a spray of flesh, bone and platinum.

The first time her mind had conjured the images of what

had happened, his fingers had come off intact...after dangling by skin. Now they exploded, flesh, blood, and pieces of his own bone lodging in distant parts of his body.

By the time heavy rolling nausea replaced the sensation short-circuit Quinn's hands closed on her shoulders to shake her out of it.

"This is why I didn't want to tell you." He demanded, "Are you sick?"

Demanded.

"Yes!" she barked in return, flinging her hands free of her face and his off her in a spike of adrenalin she'd never been so thankful for.

Anger with herself wasn't the only emotion she had a right to in this moment. He'd earned her anger too. "What else are you hiding about that?"

"Nothing."

"You know what? I don't care. I don't care. You have to go now. I want you to go. You go home." She knew she was muttering. She knew she was ranting. She became aware she was also ripping through the closet when she snatched up his jacket and slammed the door. "Clothes. You have clothes. Put on your clothes."

He took the jacket, but eyed her with such calm she wanted to hit him.

"Clothes in case the cameras followed us home. And I hope the car waited so you don't have to call a cab or hitchhike!"

"Anais..." The way he said her name proclaimed her the unreasonable one. "I didn't want to make it worse. I was cruel when I told you about it the first time."

Grabbing both shirts from the sofa, she pushed them into his arms too. "No, rather than just telling me, you did what you always do. Distracting me with sex from something you didn't want to talk about. You said we'd do better this time, but you're *still* doing it."

The difference was she wouldn't let him get away with it this time.

"We have done better. It's a process. You don't fix things overnight. Yeah, okay, maybe I screwed up, but you didn't see your face at dinner when you talked about my hand. And when I told you the first time…"

When he started pulling his shirts on, she pushed past him to head up the stairs.

"This isn't done. Be angry. That's fine. I'm not exactly happy either right now, but we'll talk tomorrow."

Rolling her eyes, she called over her shoulder to lock the door behind him, too weary from the dreadfully long day to even keep fighting about it.

CHAPTER TEN

QUINN GAVE ANAIS three days to get over being angry with him. No calling. No texting. No standing outside her house with a stereo blaring some sappy love song…

He tried to wait and be patient, and that lasted until Wednesday. The Sip was coming up and he needed this sorted out before they had to make their biggest public appearance before the wedding the following weekend.

Which was how he found himself knocking at her office door after Ben had alerted him to her presence at the facility for the first time since their divorce failure had been made public.

This time, he didn't wait or second guess, just knocked and went inside.

She sat at her desk, dressed in her uniform, a prosthetic limb on the desk and a pair of calipers in hand, checking measurements. When he closed the door, she looked up as if she'd expected him. "Hi."

"You're back at work?"

"I'm here two days this week only. They needed me to fill a couple shifts while they're scrambling to hire someone to cover my patient list until we know whether I'll be able to come back full-time." She gestured to a chair opposite her desk. "I was going to call later."

"You were?" He sat. It all seemed too easy. There wasn't that fizzing crackle about her that announced her anger today and, with the transparency of emotion in her eyes these days, that was something to take comfort in.

She gestured again with the calipers to a newspaper on the corner of her desk. "Story about the embassy party and The Sip."

"I've seen a few photos of us from that night, but no articles yet." He opened it where she directed him to read the story while she finished up with the prosthetic.

"It's pretty positive," she said and began packing up the limb.

The writer reported mundane facts about the party and general impressions of those in attendance, but finished with a quote from an unnamed source about the royal couple.

"'Princess Anais choked up when describing the harrowing days after the Prince Captain's injury and how it changed her heart...'" Quinn read out loud, then looked at her, the words leaving a bad taste in his mouth. "That's not exactly accurate. You said it changed your specialty, but this makes it sound like you heard I was hurt, realized you loved me and then magically became a good person."

For once when talking about the media, she chuckled, rising to round the desk so she could lean against it before him. "But it doesn't say I did something bad."

"You think it's positive?" He chucked the paper onto the floor and wiped his hands on his trousers, just to get that slick newspaper feel off his skin.

"It's more positive than anything else they ever wrote about me. About us."

Hearing her say *us* after a tense few post-fighting days helped a little. "I suppose. But I still don't like it. Someone putting it like that when it was personal and heartfelt. It wasn't a show. I don't like the way it's being twisted."

He was so turned inward, trying to match the words he'd read with the speaking voices of those who'd been sitting near them, he didn't notice her moving until she filled his vision and just sat across his lap.

That simple move summoned a smile he couldn't contain as their eyes met.

"You're not angry with me anymore?" he asked, holding off on wrapping his arms around her, on kissing her, until he was certain.

"I got over it last night. But I was still dreading this conversation. Be happy. The article did something else good for us besides not painting me as a horrible wretch." She wrapped one arm around his shoulders and leaned in, giving him an unspoken green light to do what his arms ached for.

"What's that?"

"Gave you the chance to say something wonderful, and complain about the press with enough heat to rival my old tirades."

He couldn't help pressing his luck. "If I write a strongly worded letter, you think you might feel moved to kiss me?"

Her answer was to press her soft lips to his, warm, lingering and loving. One kiss that lasted long enough to imprint the feel of her long after it ended and she'd leaned her forehead against his.

Cheekiness aside, he felt the words coming out before he even knew what they were going to be. "Are we okay?"

She nodded subtly. "Just don't do it again. I'd rather you hurt me than sweep everything under the rug. I get that you don't mean it that way, but it makes me feel like you don't care enough to make the effort."

"That's not—"

"I know."

He should tell her about the video. The one he hadn't watched. The one he really knew too little about to drop on her now.

She tilted her head to his shoulder and, instead of speaking, he held her closer.

He'd tell her.

After the wedding.

* * *

A wide valley ringed the base of Palace Peak, the land long devoted to sport or merrymaking related to various holidays and festivals.

In honor of The Sip—the big, traditional party given before royal weddings—massive colorful tents littered the valley in a zigzagging path toward the palace, each representing a different brand of mead made by his countrymen.

Quinn watched as, far below, people prowled from tent tavern to tent tavern, sampling each brand's mead en route to the large white pavilion at the back, where the revelers would cast their vote on the gender of their future child and await their King and his family.

He couldn't see the details from the high vantage point at the rear of the palace, but from a distance it looked like fun, like organized, colorful chaos.

Due to the popularity of the event, in his grandfather's time—when travel became much easier—it had been changed to an invitation only event rather than the free-for-all the old festival valley took years to recover from. For three generations now, a select few thousand guests were invited personally by the royal family, and a lottery system bestowed the remaining five thousand plus-one invitations, resulting in ten thousand more guests from the citizenry. Nearly fifteen thousand people waited for them below.

One big, ironically named open bar.

"Did the organizers provide safe, free transportation for our guests and extra security as I asked?"

Quinn turned at Anais's voice and felt a huge smile steal across his face. She hated the title, but in that dress…she was a princess. A princess dressed in a color he would never tire of. One sexy bared shoulder, then some manner of short, sheer blue and green ruffled silk that blended together but still hugged her slight curves.

"And food to lessen the possible drunken debauchery, Your Gorgeous Highness."

She scrunched her face at the title. "Don't forget lessening the extent of the probable poor decision-making."

How in the world had he fallen in love with a teetotaler?

"So, you're saying you don't want the gender of our first child being predicted by a bunch of lushes? Have you no respect for tradition?" He slammed his fist into the balcony balustrade to act out his faux outrage.

His antics were rewarded with a tiny smile.

"I'll believe that when you show the science behind it." She straightened his tie, his shoulders, then tugged on his tails to be certain he was ordered. "We should go down; the day's almost done and I'd like to get seated before the crowds reach to the pavilion."

She was not at all looking forward to the party. Even with the cheerful, spritely folk music dancing up from the valley below. He wouldn't even mention the toasts—drunken and sober—that had become part of the tradition. She'd stopped indicating her displeasure at the idea of staying married, but he didn't want to risk upsetting it more than tonight's spectacle would.

"Are you looking forward to the dancing? I know you've been practicing, and your dress keeps your feet visible so every drunken reprobate can marvel at your fancy stomping."

She snorted then but took his hand and tugged him back through the palace and into the carriage waiting for them.

In the light of the late afternoon, the ring on her finger shone blue-green—the perfect color, the color that had informed his decision to badger every jeweler in Europe until he'd gotten the stone he wanted of sufficient size for a proper engagement ring, but small enough she'd actually wear it.

She took his hand as she settled into the cushioned seat and the carriage started down towards the large tents.

Things had been calm between them since that day at Almsford and, as long as they got through tonight smoothly, everything would be all right. He could see the finish line; they just had to keep it together until they got there.

Hoofbeats on cobblestones announced them and the crowds parted, opening a path to the rear pavilion. She waved, as was expected, and he did as well though he kept an arm around her shoulders.

If he had any chance of giving her any ease tonight, it would be through contact. He shouldn't stop touching her. The connection helped them both, and even if he'd sworn off using distraction to soothe her, this wasn't using sex as a distraction. It didn't count.

Only when they were inside the white pavilion did Quinn's good mood falter. It was the throne that did it, the one that would stay empty tonight because the King was too ill to attend.

"What's wrong?" Anais asked from beside him at the high table. When he turned toward her, the grim and worried shadow had returned to her lovely eyes.

Don't trouble her with it yet.

Later.

"Philip's not here yet. But it's fine—he'll be in time for the toasts."

While the King wouldn't be attending at all. People would wonder why. She'd wonder why, might even take it personally—her relationship with Philip had always been good enough, but the King had kept her at a formal distance.

Telling her the truth now would just give her one more thing to be concerned about, when she should be looking like a happy bride.

"Should we have waited for him and the King to ride with us?"

The King...

He was saved from another lie by the sudden cacophony of Philip's arrival and a small army of guests behind him. "He came down earlier to try the meads and cast his vote. He's campaigning for the sweetest mead available. Although no one really believes it. Sweet meads never win the vote; everyone always thinks it should be a son born first and votes dry regardless."

"Wants a niece, does he?"

"That's what he said. What he actually said was: I'm so good at breaking traditions, I should have a girl to break the streak. Give the country a born princess to fuss over again."

There had been no daughters in the family at all since the late eighteenth century, helped by the custom of keeping families small to avoid a sprawling royal line and possible inheritance issues.

She accepted it with a little shake of her head, still untalkative. Where Philip was, order soon followed. As soon as he'd greeted them both, he took to the dais and began the formal festivities.

Toasts came—as much as they could be called toasts when it was far more like his cousins and extended family roasted him instead. By the time a lull came, the band at the far end began to play.

Anais's pointed looks toward the empty throne said more about her attention than words could have. He definitely had to tell her after the party. Truthfully, he couldn't think of why he hadn't told her before—sitting with his terminally ill grandfather had been part of his daily life since returning home.

Philip hand-delivered two tankards of the sweetest mead to them. Anais took a literal sip and went to cast her vote for the sweetest mead available.

When she returned, it was with a pallor so stark that when he saw her crossing back to him he was compelled to meet her and lead her back to her seat.

"It affected you that strongly?"

The confused look she gave him answered that question. "That tiny sip?"

She swallowed visibly and shook her head, her gaze skating over the crowd to land on a lanky, dark-haired man.

Not again.

He'd taken care of Ratliffe. The man was out of the country and would be arrested if he returned without royal decree.

Her fear, which he'd once tried to ignore, was now like a foghorn to him. It made keeping quiet a massive undertaking.

Another drink of the mead held his tongue, but he struggled to mask his frustration while watching her go from visibly stricken to breathing more evenly, and finally to where some color returned to her cheeks.

Pale and terrified to quasi-normal.

She'd reasoned through without his help. That had to be an improvement. Public appearances must be triggering them; this was the third time it had happened.

With no other weapons in his publicly acceptable arsenal, he offered her his hand and stood. When she slowly mirrored his action, he led her onto the dance floor. Distraction was all he had right now.

Only one sighting of the specter of Wayne Ratliffe tonight. Anais still didn't know if that was because afterward she'd purposely avoided looking at many people, or because the jubilant mood of the people celebrating their engagement had washed those probable hallucinations away.

She'd like to think the latter, then she could tell herself that she was getting over it. She'd like to pretend that since Ben's surgery she hadn't seen Wayne everywhere.

Well, everywhere but the American Embassy. She couldn't make any more sense of that than she could the scores of waking nightmare visions clogging her days.

They plagued her so effectively she couldn't help jumping to that conclusion about the random daily calls and hangups happening since Quinn had removed Wayne from the country. Even though her numbers were unlisted and she couldn't conceive how he'd get them.

Anais took Quinn's hand as he helped her down from the carriage which had brought them back to the palace.

He was the only good part of her evening. Nothing terrible had happened at the party, but he had been a bubble of peace in the chaos.

She wanted to stay in the bubble with him tonight. Pretend this was going to work out as much as she could no longer deny she ached for it to.

As soon as her feet settled firmly on the ground, she stepped against him and reached for him, rising on tiptoe as her arms crept around his shoulders and urged his mouth to hers. Not an ounce of resistance held him from her, his wonderful mouth pressed to hers, and soon he had his arms tight around her waist, his head tilting to deepen the kiss that had become her unspoken plea to stay.

Late in the evening, late in their relationship, and late with admissions she'd known the truth of for weeks, Anais leaned her head back just enough to give it words. She whispered against his lips, "I believe you."

The sharp intake of his breath made her open her eyes, and the intensity of the emotion she saw made her throat constrict. He nodded, accepting her words, and then immediately swept her into motion with him. One arm released her, but the other stayed around her waist as he hurried her up the long stairs through the public entrance of the palace and across the brilliantly ornate and decorated foyer to the private wing.

Practically running, his feet didn't slow until he had her alone in his suite and the door closed. With a twirl, her back touched the door and his mouth fell on hers again, the hunger of his kiss sparking over every inch of her. She even felt it in the arches of her feet.

She had questions and fears, and darkness hovered on the horizon. The country might accept her now, but once Wayne returned for real—and he would—it would come undone. But that wasn't tonight, and she needed to be close to Quinn, to soothe away the worry she'd seen on his too handsome face every time he had looked toward the empty throne. She needed to see the rest of him, the body she'd known and which was at once strange and familiar to her wandering hands.

Finding the front of his collar, she fumbled with the black bow tie until the feat of continuing to be kissed senseless while trying to untie anything became too much and she broke the kiss, tilting her head to see his tie enough to get it open, and the buttons beneath it.

Quinn shrugged out of the formal tails, tossed them onto a couch and then pulled her back into his arms.

He'd never been in bad shape, but now the man's shoulders could've been used to model anatomy for biology classes. She felt his hands wrestling with the numerous buttons up the back of her bodice, and her hands were pulled from their appreciative exploration as he spun her to face the door so he could attack the fastenings from the back.

A button or two, and he'd kiss the back of her neck, nip, bite and suck at the skin he could get at, then struggle to unwrap more of her.

Sometimes he brushed his lips so lightly over her skin goosebumps rose over her entire body.

In seven years he hadn't forgotten one thing about touching her. Even during the frenzied sex on her office floor, he couldn't help himself angling his thrusts just the right way, assaulting the most tender parts of her neck and shoulders with kisses that defined every type of kiss possible, leaving light marks on her chest for days after.

The emotion flowing off him now echoed that fervor, but was as far from that dark need as she'd been from home and from him for so many years.

When her dress finally came open and he could tug it down and off, he gave a triumphant laugh and within seconds the long-line bra she'd worn popped off too.

Only then did he let her turn back to him to resume her quest to get him out of his clothes.

"Bed this time," he croaked and she nodded, so starved for the feel of his chest she had to stop with his shirt half undone when she caught the gentle whorls of dark hair and pressed her lips to the center, then nibbled and licked her way up to his collarbone. His stuttering breaths and gasps sounded like music.

Her dress was abandoned several steps back. Panties and shoes weren't much of a barrier, so Quinn joined her fumbling efforts to tear through his clothes, and soon the shirt was gone. Her eyes went to those scars again, but this time her mouth followed—kissing each puckered ridge.

Every brush of her lips had him twisting, his breaths coming in stuttering gasps.

At the bed, he tossed her back and kicked off the rest of his clothes in mere heartbeats.

His body felt strong enough to put her faith in. Tempted her to compare that strength to his loyalty and love. But that put him out of reach; she couldn't have anything that beautiful.

He looked like a man who'd earned his strength through labor and toil, through hardship. But hardship didn't always build emotional character the way it could knit muscle.

"Any mystery left?" he asked, a flirting light in his eyes, his breathless smile brightening the need that had been roaring between them both.

Too much.

Thinking about it would ruin everything.

"Unraveling," she said instead, then laughed as he grabbed her feet and chucked her shoes over his shoulders.

By the time he'd stripped her bare patience had long been abandoned by them both, and she couldn't tell which of them was shaking hardest as he sank into her. All she knew was an exquisite ache in her chest, and the certainty that no one could ever replace him.

Fiery passion, pleasure so acute it was almost pain and raw sweetness she couldn't remember ever fully appreciating, but which she knew she didn't deserve.

At the height of it, when she'd shattered and he'd put her fragments back together again, she tugged his head onto her breast and smoothed back the damp, curling brown hair, stubbornly refusing to let those thoughts reform that had only amplified since he'd slid that beautiful ring onto her finger.

"I know you're not ready to say it," he murmured when his breaths had stopped coming in gulps, and lifted over her to look into her eyes. "But I need to say it."

Chewing her upper lip in an effort to hold back the tide building behind her eyes, she nodded and held his gaze as he said the words to her again, words she'd admitted she now believed. She still didn't deserve them, but she wanted them. Oh, how she wanted him.

A nod was the answer she could give and when he gently thumbed tears from her lashes and laid his head back down, she returned to petting his hair, knowing clearly this time that the shaking was hers.

The sweeter he was, the more certain she became he'd be snatched away from her and that she should run now, as fast and hard as her feet would carry her. The sweeter he was, the more she came to suspect she'd just had sex without barriers again because she wanted pregnancy to blame for being stupid this time. Pregnancy would make it understandable, maybe even forgivable, to stay until she was so consumed by him that his turning from her would destroy her.

But betrayal always came when least expected. He should know that almost as well as she did.

CHAPTER ELEVEN

"Wake up, sleepy."

His voice, warm and happy, broke through Anais's lazy morning sleep like a blast from the past, announcing Quinn's intention to get her up by any means necessary.

She had to work to keep the instinctive smile off her face.

"Nope."

Even as she said the word and tried to calm her cheeks, Anais felt her body tensing, readying for his attack.

It was an old game. She couldn't remember a day he hadn't woken up in a good mood—something she'd have sworn she hated before Quinn. But somehow, even when she wasn't legitimately reluctant to rise, she found herself playing along, which always improved her natural morning crankiness. Quinn's improvised wake-up techniques were more effective than coffee, both for her alertness level and her mood.

Sweet kisses.

Ear-nibbling.

Forehead-licking…

He'd even bitten her toes a time or two.

Once, he'd bitten her bum and turned his wake-up call into the best morning sex in history.

"Get up. Get up," he chanted, bouncing the bed a couple of times so that she jiggled in the covers. Then stopped.

Was that it?

She squeezed her eyes tighter shut, conscious now of the distinct possibility that, good mood or not, he just didn't *do* that anymore. In which case…yeah, she'd just be lying there, looking like a childish, lazy moron.

He'd stopped talking. She didn't hear moving either… Had he gone? Had he gone and she'd missed it?

The instant she opened her eyes to check he pounced, ripping the bedclothes back until she was bared to the hips. Then he loosed a battle cry, hands lifting with fingers curled in a classic *Gotcha!* position.

He. Was. Going. To. Tickle. Her.

Tickling. Morning tickling?

Before she could process it, he took a breath deep enough to puff his cheeks and launched himself at her belly.

One arm clamped over her thighs, the other wrapped over her chest to lock her arm down. Secured, he pressed his mouth to her belly and blew hard, unleashing the loudest, rudest noises into the room and sending those deep tissue vibrations through her.

Anais yelped, tried not to laugh, and did the only thing she could: squirm hard to get free.

But it didn't matter how hard she tried not to laugh or get away, she soon shook with the kind of crippling, uncontainable laughter that rendered her body useless.

When every breath sounded like a tortured asthmatic's he'd stop and let her get a lungful. Or maybe he just stopped to refill his own lungs, needing the air to continue his onslaught.

One of her wild bucks managed to free an arm, and she shoved at his head while helplessly laughing, yelling, *"Stop!"* and turning it into a seventeen-syllable word.

He did. Just backed right off, as if he'd marked a task off his morning to-do list. "Morning," he greeted, as if none of that had just happened, and leaned down to kiss her while brushing her thoroughly messy hair from her face.

Gentle. Tender. Loving. Addictive. Especially to someone like her who'd never belonged anywhere. But she felt as if she belonged with him. When they were alone, she felt as if she belonged with him, even *to* him in a primitive way that offended her feminist sensibilities. It was just the rest of his world she couldn't even imagine fitting into.

"The sunlight gave it away." Her voice came out far huskier than she could've done on purpose. She cleared her throat and asked, "How many cups of coffee have you had?"

Even if her role required her to be the reasonable one, she couldn't keep herself from petting him while she reasserted some reason into the morning. She loved raking her fingers through his messy curling hair.

"None."

"And not hungover, I see."

"Just on sweet, sweet lovin'."

She laughed again. "Perhaps still a little drunk."

"Just on sweet, sweet—"

Clapping a hand over his mouth was the only sensible way to stop this silliness, but nothing could stop her smiling. "Slept well then?"

Behind her hand, he nodded, his eyes merry.

"Have a plan for the day you're eager to get going with?"

Wrapping one hand around her wrist, he pulled her hand free. "Hungry. We're having breakfast in bed, but not until you're no longer naked."

Winking, he slid off her, leaving her aware that he was actually dressed—if pajama bottoms counted as dressed. He certainly wasn't naked.

She sat up and he tossed a tee shirt at her, which she dutifully whisked over her head and stuffed her arms into. "I wouldn't want to come between you and your oatmeal."

"Eggs. Bacon. Fruit. No oatmeal." He opened the door of the bedroom and gestured; she heard a rolling cart and tucked the blanket around her legs so she didn't look naked save for Quinn's desert camouflage tee.

"And after you eat?" She should bring up what she'd

meant to say last night before she'd ended up throwing herself at him in the courtyard.

He said quiet thanks to the lovely person who'd brought them food, then wheeled to the bed to join her. "After I eat, I'm going to sit with Grandfather."

She'd plucked up a slice of crisp bacon and had it to her mouth before his quiet words registered. *The subject.* With it came understanding, though she'd mostly worked it out last night. "How bad is it?"

"Ten." He lost the bright playful spark from only moments before, and his shoulders came down just a little. "Ten on a scale of ten."

"Is it…? Are you…?" The words refused to take shape. It seemed traitorous somehow to ask how long before the King died. Even phrasing it as grandfather to a grandson who loved him and couldn't be bearing up well against the coming end.

"He's stable right now, but his kidneys have failed and he's too old for a transplant." Over the next few minutes, and in as few words as he could get away with, Quinn outlined the severity of his grandfather's illness, the reason he'd not been at the party and how soon after the wedding they might be having a coronation.

"He's usually awake late morning, early afternoon, so I visit with him then and go to see Ben after."

"I'm so sorry." Pathetic words.

Corrachlean had been lucky with her monarchs; they'd had it good for so long that each new king came to the throne with the respect and love of his people as a starting position. No need to win the people over or prove himself. No matter how things had gone with her marriage, and they had never gone well, that loyal and even loving feeling for King Thomas had never left her. "You could've told me before now. You told me about Ben."

"At first I didn't because we were at odds. Then I didn't because you've already been stressed over our courtship.

Last night, I regretted not telling you before you were in a position to notice he wasn't around, but by then I didn't want to put a damper on an evening already filled with things you dislike: drinking and more drinking."

She looked at the plate she'd been munching from, but abandoned it in favor of a strong cup of tea. "Would you like me to come with you this morning? I brought a change of clothes with me. I could make myself presentable. But if he wouldn't want me to, please don't feel like you can't say no."

"He actually already asked to see you yesterday at our visit. I was working up to telling you." A tiny smile followed the admission.

She leaned over to kiss him, doing all she could to avoid bringing up their past relationship and trying not to think about how it would resume. "I probably won't say much; I don't want to interrupt your visit."

"No, I mean he wants to see you privately, love. I'll take you down, but after that I'm not invited."

"Why?"

"He said he wanted to talk about some things."

"That's not at all ominous…"

She liked that she didn't need to explain why it made her nervous.

"It'll be fine. You're not being called to task by the headmaster. He's not…" There, words seemed to fail him and he shook his head. "He's different. You'll see."

If things hadn't felt real at the party, standing with Quinn outside the King's private quarters did.

King Thomas had been the hardest sell to their marriage. Anais hadn't been so foolish as to be surprised by this, but she'd thought he'd come around when he saw how much she loved his grandson. He hadn't.

But, to be fair, he had an unruly, uncontrollable grandson whose behavior jeopardized royal stability, and she'd been a huge example of that.

He'd never been unkind exactly, but always disapproving. Disapproving enough to make it abundantly clear that
she'd never fit into the family. Never be acceptable. Accepted. She'd even imagined him gleeful when he'd finally
ordered their divorce.

Illness changed people, and Quinn had said as much.
The best she could do would be to approach him as if she'd
never known him, pretend there wasn't a difficult history
there. Let him reject her afresh!

Holding Quinn's left hand, she walked behind him into
the room after the little knock announced them.

"Grandfather?"

A stately leather wingback faced the morning sun
streaming through open French windows, the only source
of light in the quiet room. A hand lifted, indicating where
he sat, right where Quinn apparently expected him to be—
they were already heading in that direction.

"Good morning." Quinn took his grandfather's translu-
cent hand and gave it a little loving jiggle before ushering
her into his line of sight. "I brought her. Don't give her too
much grief. I still have to get her to the altar. No scaring
her off for another week."

He reserved a wink for her, driving home the notion that
he was teasing, but he still kissed her cheek and all but put
her into a chair opposite the King so she couldn't run away.

"Good morning, Your Highness." She never knew how
to address the man. In her eleven-month marriage, she'd
never made any attempt to come closer than formal titles.

Pale gray eyes met hers and she managed a smile, even
as her training kicked in and she began taking inventory of
his symptoms. It gave her a controlled center to start from
when she didn't know what else was coming at her.

Flushed.

Weak.

Tired.

Quinn closed the door behind him, leaving her alone with her monarch.

"My son tells me you're to be wed at week's end. I regret that I won't be there to see either of my sons marry."

The words tilted in her mind a little. Quinn and Philip were his grandsons. Was that a symptom? Or was this a shorthand way of referring to the true state their relationship had grown into after the death of their father, the King's actual son?

"That's what I'm told too." She chuckled. "I've not been involved in any of the plans. Quinn said there are wedding planners who are seeing to everything, and they've had such short notice. I'm sure I'll be more than impressed with whatever they manage. The gown I know is far too beautiful for me to do justice."

"Nonsense, Mireille, I'm sure you'll look more beautiful than even Nicholas could imagine."

Mireille and Nicholas—Quinn's parents.

Symptom.

"I'll do my best and, if I fail, he'll still humor me." She stood up and slipped over to his side. "May I kiss your cheek, King Thomas?"

He tilted his head back, pale eyes smiling. Permission, even if he thought her someone else. Anais pressed her lips to his cheek and felt the heat that explained the flush and his confusion.

"You're warm," she said as clearly as she could, crouching down beside him in the light spilling through the windows. When she had his eye, she saw the instant the fog lifted and he recognized her. Right behind it, he realized his earlier confusion.

"Oh, dear, Anais, I thought..." His voice trailed off as his mind caught up.

She took his hand and smiled despite the tears she felt in her eyes again. "You have a fever, sir. You're not losing your senses. It's the fever. May I look at the port? I want to make sure it's not inflamed."

Although he would never have allowed such familiarity before, he squeezed her hand, then rolled up the long sleeve on his pajamas to reveal an AV graft in his upper arm. She didn't need the bright sunshine to see how red the skin was.

"Does it hurt right now, sir?"

"It's tender," he admitted and then laid his head back. "I asked you here to apologize for the way your marriage was received. You two acted on blind love, and I only saw breach of protocol and tradition, another instance where my grandson bent to impulse and whimsy. But once it was done…"

"You're not to blame for that."

"We're all to blame for it, I expect. That's how these things go. People don't fall from a single mistake; they fall from many." He reached up and patted her cheek and her heart fisted up, so tight she almost choked on it. Couldn't even name the flood of emotions that traveled with the tears in her eyes.

Sympathy? Worry for him? For Quinn? Gratitude at his sudden acceptance? All of it.

"He's going to need you, when the time comes."

Words that sounded like his blessing.

She twisted her mouth to the side, keeping it together long enough to offer words of comfort and gratitude, then a promise to look at his medical record and see what antibiotics would help.

No longer able to control the tears threatening, she kissed his cheek again and excused herself.

Quinn had told her what another infection would mean. And now she had to tell him.

Even had it been the longest hallway in the palace rather than the shortest, she couldn't have stopped crying before she got there.

* * *

"What do you mean he's in and out?" Quinn nearly shouted, then realized his volume. With a deep breath, he rolled his shoulders and eased down into the chair he'd abandoned with Philip on the business side of the King's desk.

Her red-rimmed eyes were clarification enough, but he couldn't accept it.

"He's experiencing moments of confusion," she said gently. "It's not dementia. It's probably the fever, but it's also possible he needs another round of dialysis sooner than expected. Toxins that build up in the blood can cause confusion. But he realized it; I didn't correct him when he called me Mireille and Quinn Nicholas. Then he recognized me."

"Mom?" Philip asked. He'd been looking far too calm for this conversation, but alarm edged into his voice upon hearing their grandfather had called his granddaughter-in-law by the name of his long-dead daughter-in-law.

"We'll just have to talk him into another placement," Quinn said. "Or will antibiotics clear it up?"

"I'm honestly not sure. I think once they get infected, it's hard to treat them without moving."

Her voice was so gentle it made it all worse. She was preparing him for the worst; every note of sympathy in her voice drove him that much closer to losing it.

"They've done three now?" she asked, looking at his grandfather's medical record. "Did they not want to try a fistula? They take a while to mature for use, but they don't get infected as often as grafts."

Philip reached for his phone. "They tried that initially, but it wasn't maturing as they needed it to."

"I don't know what that is." Quinn knew he should have learned everything about kidney failure too. He could've been reading that when he'd sat by hospital beds. And he'd do that after he put a stop to this. "I'm going to talk to him."

Anais stepped around the desk and clutched his arm to

stop him. "He needs to rest, Quinn. Go sit with him, but don't fight with him."

"That's all I've been doing since I got home, Anais. I've spent damned near a month trying, with varying degrees of success, to make two people I love want to live. Three, if you count you."

Quinn watched her retreat immediately, first the warmth he always needed from her, then her hands, finally her whole body—she stepped back from him and he didn't know if it was anger or hurt that propelled her.

He was being unreasonable, unfair even, to lump her in with Ben and Grandfather when her version of giving up on life was entirely metaphorical compared to theirs. But he couldn't apologize to soften his stance right now. Fire got things done.

Pounding back down the hallway with Philip on his heels, Quinn let himself into his grandfather's room. "You've got an infection, Grandfather. We're going to get the doctor here to schedule you for another graft. And antibiotics." He looked up at Philip. "You should go call the doctor."

"I did it while you were shouting at Anais," Philip muttered and then sat down opposite the King. "You're not going to feel better until the infection is taken care of. I think they can do another temporary site while this one heals…"

"No."

Until now, the King had been placidly listening to them both, but when Philip suggested treatment Quinn wasn't aware of—because he'd been in another damned country—it got a response, but not the right one.

What would get the right response? With Ben, he'd had Rosalie to use as a motivator, but their grandmother had long since passed away.

"Temporary access site sounds like a good thing." Quinn fumbled along to back Philip up. "Infections are a nasty way to die. I don't… I don't want you to die like that."

His throat closed on the words so that he had to take a few runs at it.

"I doubt any death is particularly pleasant, sweet boy. I'm just sorry I'm not going to be around for your wedding and to meet my first great-grandchild."

That sounded like goodbye. As if he were dying today. Or as if he needed to say things before the fever robbed him of his senses for good.

Quinn couldn't accept that. He'd never argued with his grandfather, or hadn't since his age had ended in *teen*, but he argued now. "You can be around for that."

"It's not your decision, Quinn." Philip's gentle rebuke set his hackles rising.

He stood and rounded on Philip, every instinct saying *fight*. "You're so ready for the crown you're ready to give up to a little infection?"

"That's not fair. I've been here…"

"And I've been somewhere I had to fight every day to keep people I love alive. I even had to fight to keep people I hated alive. You expect me to just sit back and let death take *him* when there are things we can do to prevent it?" He was yelling. He didn't mean to be yelling. Again. He'd just yelled at Anais…whom he couldn't find in the room. She hadn't come with them, wasn't there to see him losing it.

"Quinton."

His softly spoken name sucked the rage out of him and his strength with it. He felt it in the wobble of his knees and sat back down before they buckled. "Yes?"

"Philip hasn't given up at the first obstacle. He's been here through the other moves. That's nothing against you, but to you—who has just now been able to come home to us—this feels like the first."

He knew that. Logically, he knew it. But the idea of losing someone now that he'd finally gotten them back…

A dust mote swirled in a beam of sunshine from the open windows, and he just let himself watch. It was better than watching his grandfather giving up. It even felt kind of applicable—watching it drift into the shadow and invisibility that might as well be nothingness.

"I can give you one more move if you can give me something."

The words were the first iota of hope since he'd awakened with Anais's soft hair on his skin, and it yanked his attention back. "What can I give you?"

"Your word that with the next failure you will accept my decision."

He froze. Maybe the next time it would last longer. Long enough for Quinn to come up with an argument that would work. Hope was hope.

How long had the last move held? He should know that too. The King expected his infection to return soon, to not last as long as Quinn needed him to last.

"If I say no, you let yourself be eaten by this infection now?"

A nod was his answer.

There was no choice.

Despite the cold emptiness opening in his chest, Quinn nodded. It was still a win.

So why did it leave him feeling empty…and guilty?

Grandfather forcing bitter terms wasn't the same as him forcing Anais to say yes to the wedding. They would have a long, great, love-filled life together. Children. Unruly teenagers. Grandchildren. Maybe even great-grandchildren. Good things would come from *his* act of coercion.

It wasn't the same.

God, Anais hated the penthouse, but she'd had a last-minute dress fitting and it was the easiest place to do it.

Now done, Anais sat alone on his sofa, waiting for Quinn to get home. Her eyes kept skirting to the bedroom where the safe was. She couldn't remember the combination to the safe, probably the only reason she hadn't come for those pictures the day after he'd told her about them.

In days they were getting married, but she was rapidly unspooling. No work now; all she had to do was spend time at home, thinking of all the ways this could come undone. She stayed because she needed Quinn to help her shore up the crumbling walls around what remained of her sanity if they were going to make it to the church.

"Hey," Quinn said, drawing her attention away from the direction of the safe and alerting her to his arrival at once.

Before she could say anything the smile dropped from his handsome face. "What happened?"

Lots. Sort of.

"I need you to talk me through something," she said haltingly, because she'd just sat there when she should've been coming up with the best, most calm, rational way to start this conversation. Yet more proof she was losing her mind.

Quinn approached slowly; she must look as skittish as she felt. "Okay… What?"

"Your plans. Like 'Break in Case of Emergency' plans for the whole… Wayne comes back and shows his copies to everyone—including the King, who only just began accepting the idea of you marrying me a few days ago."

"Four days," Quinn said instead, settling carefully beside her. "You just have to make it four more days. Then things will calm down."

"That's not a plan." She laughed, too high and fast to sound like anything but panic. "You don't have an emergency plan, do you?"

"My plan is to keep tabs on him so he can't do anything like that, and it's working just fine."

"That's not a plan. That's hoping. Vigorous hoping maybe, but I'm talking about an evacuation plan for when the building catches on fire, and you're counting on the presence of a smoke detector to prevent fires from starting."

"What happened?" he asked again, his voice so calm it increased her alarm.

"I know you think you've taken care of Wayne." She felt her voice rising and tried to calm it, tried to speak more slowly. "It's been happening since the park. I know, or I think, and try to tell myself it's never him. How could it be him when I see him everywhere? That's not logical, and I remind myself of that, but I don't *know* that for sure. One of them could actually be him, but instead I convince myself ten times a day that I'm just losing my mind, which isn't helping either."

Not level. Not calm. One moment her voice was in the rafters, the next the bottom of the ocean...because she kept babbling. She hadn't meant to just subject him to a panic attack.

"Ten times a day?"

"I don't know, exactly. I don't keep count. I just see him. He might be in another country, but you can't be sure of that. He could still surface. He could have copies. He could wait years, wait until he runs out of money, then come back at us. How can we live with this and not have an emergency plan? What would you tell the King?"

As soon as it was out of her mouth, Anais knew she'd chosen the wrong example. The King wouldn't be here in years.

The grim line his mouth became confirmed the misstep.

"I'm sorry. I wasn't thinking." She tried to undo it before he got too upset about that to be logical about this. "It's just when I saw King Thomas, he made me feel like family for the first time. If just for a few minutes, it made me afraid to lose that. And, now that I say it out loud, I see it's not even about everyone else. It's you too. I'm going crazy because I'm afraid of losing you once you've seen them."

He scrubbed at his forehead. Didn't work, but his frustration with her couldn't be worse than the frustration she felt for herself.

"I'm not going to leave you over dirty pictures I already know exist."

"Knowing and seeing are different things. You can't know it won't change the way you see me." She felt her temperature rising and stood up; maybe moving would help. "It was over a decade ago and it still affects the way I see myself!"

"How much more than a decade?"

The slow tilt of his head with the lowering of his brows set off alarms in her chest.

When she didn't say anything, he tried again, and this time he did stand up. "How old were you, Anais?"

"Old enough to know better," she muttered. "Does it matter?"

"You're twenty-seven. Over a decade ago? Yeah, that damn well matters."

Not the point she was getting at. Anais wasn't even sure what her point had been before, but this conversation was doing nothing for that fear she'd been trying to ignore. "What matters is that I'm afraid all the time. It's not just my paranoid hallucinations... I'm getting calls. He calls, waits for me to answer, hangs up. Happens on my cell, at home too."

"That could be anyone. People just wanting to hear your voice."

"Or it could be *him*." Unraveling—the whole thing was unraveling, harder and faster, the more they talked. And it felt exactly like she'd imagined the Wayne blackmail conversation going seven years ago.

"Just listen," he said, making a clear effort to modulate his voice, even taking her hand, which usually helped. "I can come up with a plan, but it's not necessary right now. I didn't just remove him from the country under controlled custody. First, I had our cyber force search of his Internet footprint. Emails. Cloud storage. Everything. We did new passwords, wiped everything clean. Found nothing online, just what he'd stashed at his mother's place, and I took both of those cameras."

He said some other things… Anais could see Quinn's mouth moving, but a loud, persistent ringing in her ears covered the sounds coming out of his mouth.

Both cameras?

Two cameras.

Why would the cameras that took the pictures matter? Camera. It was one camera.

"It was just photos," she said, or tried to say. Her voice didn't even sound over the ringing in her ears. "What does the camera…? What do you mean?"

Still ringing. And her fingers went so cold they felt stiff. Stress was causing her to have a freaking stroke.

But her vision was crystal-clear. She must've managed the words, because she saw Quinn's face lose the angry color he'd built up, and his mouth stopped moving too.

It took him a while to start talking again, which was fine considering the state of her *stroke*.

Some deep breathing slowed her heart down enough for the ringing to decrease.

He'd started talking again. Something, something… *watched enough to confirm*…something.

Watched?

Watched.

"Video?" she asked, finally hearing her own voice over the ringing.

His slow, short nod came before more words, words of increasing clarity. "After the wedding. You can do whatever you want with it."

There was a video.

She scrambled to remember. How much had she drank?

A lot. More than she could handle, but Quinn had said he'd confirmed it was her…

"There wasn't a video. That's not me—it's someone else."

"It's you."

His quiet voice did more to convince her than anything in her memory could, but still her head kept shaking. *No.* Just no. Air was becoming an issue…she breathed faster, now through her mouth as her nose couldn't keep up with the demands her lungs made.

"You need to sit down before you faint," he said, and she couldn't argue with the diagnosis. She did feel faint, but she needed air.

Only after she got the balcony door open and the cool evening air blew in did she turn back to him, still panting.

In her wildest imaginings she'd always had that argument in the back of her mind. She'd thought she could say: *That's not me. Just some excellent photo editing…* It was done all the time for a reason, but video? Could video be edited like that?

Didn't seem like it.

"I can't do this." The words came out and she bent forward to brace her hands on her knees.

"You can. I have it. It's secure. No one will see it. But, even if someone did, it's not great, but it's not the end of the world. Everyone has sex. You may have picked horribly, but everyone will get over it. Including me."

"You're not listening." She went ahead and put her head between her knees, going silent as she focused on trying to control that part of her brain that shrieked: *Run!*

He was saying something but she couldn't listen and think, and she had to think. There had to be options. Some option that let her stay with him.

"Let's not get married!" she cried, standing up, feeling the panic again in eyes she could hardly even blink they were opened so wide. "Let's just finish the divorce and then…just stay together. I could live with that. It's unconventional but, as a princess, as a wife, they wouldn't ever let it go. But as a mistress? They'd practically expect me to have a sex tape or…whatever it is. I could live with just being together."

"I couldn't." He sprang from the sofa, but didn't chase after her. "I hate that this hurts you, hate that it scares you, but you're going to have to accept a minimal amount of risk in this. You have more chance of catastrophe by car than catastrophe by Ratliffe at this point. You're my wife. Even if you refuse the wedding. You were right; it's just a display—you're my wife already and that's not changing. All this will be easier once the ceremony is over."

"I'll never have another moment's peace if we go through with this."

"Do you think you will if you leave me again at this point? How will the media react to that? If he had copies—which I would bet the crown against—when would be a better time to come forward with them than when my threats could no longer be counted on?"

She shook so hard it even felt as if her eyes trembled. Why didn't he see it? And then she got angry, and it was so much better than the panic. "Why stop there? If you're going to threaten me, go on and threaten to give them the video yourself."

Quinn's head jerked back and, in that instant, she knew his threats had been empty this whole time. Funny, it didn't come as any sort of relief. The damage was done.

He wouldn't meet her in the middle still. He couldn't love her all that much. This wasn't killing *him*.

Twisting off her ring, she gingerly placed it onto the new coffee table.

Before he could lob another empty threat, she grabbed her handbag and hurried to the door.

She really hated his penthouse. Every time she came there, it felt more and more like a mausoleum.

CHAPTER TWELVE

THE DOOR CLOSED quietly behind Anais, and Quinn couldn't do anything but stand there and stare—first at the door, then at the engagement ring he'd so carefully picked out for her all those years ago, like another target on his new metal and stone coffee table.

Muscles across his shoulders and down his arms twitched with readiness, tempting him to attack it as she had the last one, but before he could cross the room for the weapon that burst of violent energy left him and he dropped to sit on the thing instead.

When he'd come into the room, he'd known it was about to go up in flames, but it had been his own frustration that had lit the spark. His mouth. Four more days and he could've handled this entirely differently. Everything would've been okay because he wouldn't have had to look for ways to relieve her fear *and* get her to the altar too. But tonight... he hadn't known which one to focus on. Looked like he'd picked wrong.

He needed solutions.

She loved him. She'd all but admitted it and, even if it would've been nice for her to say it once this whole time, he knew it without the words.

Rosalie had been the weapon to use on Ben, because he loved her.

His pain had worked on Grandfather, also based on love.

But not Anais. Why not her?

She'd been upset when she'd rung him earlier, asking to meet him, but, like a big dumb ostrich, he'd decided to assume she was just having another harmless Ratliffe episode and wanted to see him for comfort. He didn't even think breaking up had been on her mind until he'd let the video slip…after he'd failed once again to present solutions when she'd reached out to him.

When was he going to stop doing that?

He replayed the conversation in his mind, looking for something he might have missed. Tonight—he needed solutions tonight. Tomorrow she might speak to the press and the wedding really would be off.

His heart jerked and began to pound. With shaking hands, he grabbed the engagement ring off the table and slid it onto the upper segment of his left middle finger—the finger he'd intended to wear his wedding ring. It helped somehow. Not as much as her hand in his helped every other time he was upset, but…

She'd already been upset, but she must have thought there had to be a solution or she wouldn't have started the conversation.

Or maybe she'd just been imagining how it could go down from any destructive angle she could, dreaming up new ways to terrify herself. She hadn't yet had time to process the knowledge of the video. His chest squeezed as the ghostly image of her foundered around the living room. Even when she'd talked about his hand, she hadn't been that…broken by it.

What was on that video?

His gaze slid across the miles of white that seemed to stretch between him and the bedroom.

Not watching it, not looking at the pictures, had seemed like the respectful thing to do. That was what he'd told himself. Now it seemed like another instance of him ignoring problems so he didn't have to deal with them.

Even the thought of watching it made his skin crawl.

The video's very existence had annoyed him since he'd learned about it, and it had taken three shots of rum to soothe his rage after he'd watched only enough to verify that it had been Anais on the film.

Ten years ago, she'd have been seventeen, and he'd assumed she'd been that or older then. Over a decade? Best case scenario was sixteen. Sixteen.

Sending Ratliffe too far away for him to drive over and beat him to death tonight might have been the best decision he'd made since coming home.

With a churning stomach, he forced himself into the bedroom, and through the deafening clicks of the safe dial. Portable hard drive in hand, he loaded it on his computer.

The yellow indoor light on the dingy white walls in the video did nothing to detract attention from the girl drinking and grimacing from the tumbler of dark liquid in her hand. He'd hoped maybe she'd only been so recognizable because he'd been looking for her, and hyper-alert to the situation the first time he'd turned it on, but she was unmistakable.

"Is this alcohol?" she asked.

Ratliffe confirmed, while taunting her in the same breath. Would she prefer a kiddie cocktail? Chocolate milk maybe?

Damn, that was slick…

The look on her face as she stared at the drink, first weighing her options and then determined. The way she looked at him said she was on to him, but she still went along with it, drinking it and asking for another.

Why?

If she'd been sixteen, he'd be surprised. It felt wrong and dirty to watch it now, knowing that the evening had at least gone as far as nudity. His skin squeezed too tight for his body, almost as viciously as his stomach squeezed.

What was teenage Anais getting out of any of this?

Pausing the video, he went ahead to the bar and poured himself a rum. Was this how she'd used the drink, to deaden herself to whatever she'd been going to do? Had she come to the apartment just to take pictures?

He didn't want to watch it.

He took the bottle with him back to the desk, knowing it wouldn't be his last for the night. When he'd downed the shot, he sat and started the video again.

She talked very little, but Wayne went on about exploits he obviously thought would impress her. *Wrong.* That wasn't her impressed face.

The man refilled her glass when she asked, then trotted out a camera to show her.

Still staying…for some reason he couldn't understand. The more she drank, the less bored she looked, but she still didn't look as if she liked him at all, but she *did* fake it. She twirled her hair around one finger. Anais wasn't a hair-twirler.

Forced flirting. As if she'd read "twirl your hair" in a *How to Flirt* book.

Another surge of rage raised the hairs on the back of his neck and he took another drink of the rum, watching the scene unfold before him.

Over the next twenty minutes, she went from quiet kid with her first drink, to obviously drunk and *desperate* for Ratliffe's approval.

By the time the man joined her on the bed and Anais's clothes started coming off Quinn understood why it had happened. She'd said it to him a million times, but all those times it had sounded like such an inconsequential thing to him. Not something Anais, his strong, brilliant wife, could really be hurt by.

"I don't fit."

"They won't accept me."

"The only thing that's ever been acceptable about me is my intelligence."

"You can't know that it won't change the way you see

me. It was over a decade ago and it still affects the way I see myself!"

That one hurt the most because she was right; it did change things. Just not the way she thought.

It took an hour to speed through the rest, through rum and tears he grew too bereft to fight.

She'd posed while entirely nude, but was so innocent Ratliffe had to tell her how to show her body. He even arranged her on the bed at times. Eventually put the camera down and kissed her.

And she threw up immediately, all over the man's lap.

He almost smiled, but then she passed out and his gut returned to churning while he waited to see what Ratliffe would do. He wasn't that much older than her, but at that age…a few years made a big difference. He was more worldly, obviously. Seedier…

Quinn sped through, not relaxing at all until the man went to sleep beside her, and when she finally stirred Quinn choked on his own relief and slowed the video again.

She slid out of the bed, got up, got her clothes.

By the time Ratliffe woke and began making demands—talking about what she *owed* him—she was ready to go.

He blocked her path. Reached for her.

Quinn regretted the rum; his stomach lurched as he helplessly watched her scan the room for an escape.

It was just a room in a flat. Ratliffe blocked the only door.

She looked to the side, grabbed something and, without hesitation, smashed into his face.

The screen went strange and he realized his hands were latched onto the laptop, squeezing, as if he could reach in and grab her out.

What had she grabbed?

He forced his hands off the screen and the display smoothed back out.

Alcohol bottle—Quinn identified the weapon, then the transition. She'd gone from child to adult in that second.

Ratliffe staggered forward, his hands covering his cheek, blood running through his fingers, and she ran.

Not how he'd expected the video to end. Through his shock, he couldn't help but feel proud of her.

She'd given him that scar. The scar that people would ask him about for the rest of his miserable life.

Wasted booze. No sex. Puked on. And a lifelong scar? Yeah, that'd cause a wicked grudge. And Quinn hadn't known anything about their interactions when Ratliffe had come after her for money. In the retelling, she'd sanitized it, and he'd been so wrapped up in the revelation he hadn't asked. And he'd let him go. Sent him on his way with money, even—something else for him to fix.

The video told him something else. She had it in her to fight for them, but she'd spent so long fighting for herself she probably didn't know how to do anything but try and stay safe. Apply the lesson she'd learned.

Weight seemed to press down on the back of his neck and Quinn sagged into his chair as another realization hit him; he dropped his head into his hands.

He couldn't force or coerce her into this.

He had to sign the papers.

The clock had long past struck midnight by the time Quinn had stopped reeling enough to think straight and start moving again.

Detective called, reports—minimal as they were—gathered, Ratliffe was still in his new flat in his new country.

Though he'd been unable to even contemplate sleep, he had managed to stop drinking in time to be sober enough to drive by eight the next morning, the absolute latest minute he could wait to go to her.

Sharon answered the door almost as soon as he rang the bell, the first thing he'd been thankful for in nearly fourteen hours.

"Oh, no, Quinton Corlow. The last time you came, you

said you weren't going to upset her, but you did. If you want to talk to my daughter, you can do it through a lawyer."

She shoved at the door and he braced his shoulder against it. "Wait. I brought something Anais will want." He lifted the bedraggled yellow envelope and held it up to the narrow opening so Sharon could see it. Divorce papers.

Hope was the only thing keeping him upright—that and a plan only an idiot would take comfort in.

It took a few tense seconds, but she begrudgingly opened the door and let him inside, calling over her shoulder, "Anais, Prince Quinton is here."

Score one for Team Hope. Now just a few more...

Quinn followed the direction Sharon called and, to his surprise, Anais came around a corner from what he could only assume was the direction to the kitchen, considering the apron covering her torso and the flour dusting it.

"You're baking?" He couldn't help the question; he'd never really witnessed her doing much at all in the kitchen. She made an occasional burnt grilled cheese, but...

"I do that sometimes."

As she neared, he could see from the circles under her red puffy eyes that she'd not slept either.

Another spark of hope.

"Can we talk?"

He breathed as slowly as he could, and hoped he didn't pass out from lack of oxygen. She needed his confidence, even if it was a big fat lie right now.

She led the way up the stairs, another thing to be thankful for—this would be hard enough without his mother-in-law giving him the evil eye.

Once they'd stepped into her meticulously clean bedroom, he went to the desk, pulled out the chair and sat. Maybe that would help his agitated body need less oxygen. Also, his roiling stomach made it hard to keep steady on his feet.

Give her what she wants, then give her a reason to fight for them.

"You haven't gone to the press yet, have you?"

She stopped in the middle of the room and wrapped her arms around herself the way he itched to. "I assumed you'd want to do that."

Want to.

He sucked in a deep breath and felt his cheeks puff as he let it back out. "It's probably better if all marriage announcements come through the palace."

It was as diplomatic as he could be without lying to her, and he wasn't going to lie to her. Not today. No matter how much easier it would be to make up some story about Ratliffe meeting an untimely and wholly satisfying "accident."

She swayed on her feet, and he noticed she still wore yesterday's clothing. Another nod to hope.

Give her what she wants.

Opening the battered envelope, he extracted the documents he knew she'd recognize, and held them out to her. "I signed them and checked with the attorney to make sure they're still viable."

She watched with uneasiness and pain he'd give the rest of his hand for the opportunity to soothe away.

"When will you file them?"

Give her a reason to fight for them.

"I'm not," he said and, when she didn't take them, he laid them with the envelope on her desk and turned back to her. "I'm leaving them for you to file."

"Oh." She braced for the hit he had to throw.

He'd do it while looking her in the eye, but he wouldn't crowd her. He stood.

"I'm not doing this because I want a divorce. I don't ever want to be apart from you. You deserve more than some sketchy mistress situation. You *deserve* to be my wife, Anais. We *deserve* to have a family together. But I can't force you into this. Grandfather has my will held hostage by a promise, and it feels…"

"Bad," she softly supplied when his words faltered.

"And like he's not really living, even though the temporary port is fine until the new graft heals enough to use. Not living, just breathing. Existing. I don't want that for you. I don't want you afraid and unhappy, even if it means I get to have you with me."

She shifted on her feet, her arms staying around her body though her hands pulled away, flexing and rolling at the wrist. Tense. "Thank you. That's kinder than I deserve."

The words hurt. "No, baby." His voice broke and her eyes—those eyes he so loved—snapped to meet his, then widened at the tears he felt wetting his cheeks.

Make her fight for them.

Pulling the portable USB drive from his pocket, he let himself cross to her. Taking her hand almost broke him. It might be the last time she let him touch her, and he might be wasting it. Turning her hand over, he placed the storage device on her palm.

"The photos are in the envelope. I didn't look at them."

Her hand shook.

"But I did watch the video."

Color drained from her face and she stepped back. "Why?" She would've pulled away if he hadn't held fast, needing to keep the connection. It was the only thing that prevented that sharp knife he felt at his throat from carving into him.

"I needed to know what I was fighting. I've been doing what you and Philip both said I do—waiting for things to work out. You didn't know what to tell people—to tell our children—if it came to public scrutiny. I do now."

The short, soft, mirthless laugh said *nothing could excuse this.*

He tugged enough to get her closer so he could say words that should never be shouted.

"I'd say that feeling alone is terrible for anyone, let alone a child, but you were still strong enough to fight through it. I'd say an evil man hurt you, but you got away and never let it keep you from becoming the amazing woman you are. I'd say…we all make bad decisions when we're hurting, and that's the reason you can't let people stay alone. That's why we fight for people we love. That's why we fight for people who can't fight for themselves."

Her bitter, teary expression became wary again, then just closed.

"You need to watch it," he whispered through a tight throat and let go of her hand. "But not alone. I really don't want to see it again, but I'll watch it with you if you need me."

She'd heard him, because she looked at the drive as if to make sure it was still in her hand.

"I don't need to watch it. I remember everything."

"I don't think you do, or you're just holding that girl to impossible standards."

She closed her hand over the drive, her chin falling as she stared at it.

"How old were you?"

"It was the week of my sixteenth birthday," she answered, but didn't look like she knew why she had.

Days before the age of consent. It didn't really matter—there was no way for him to make that right, but it did ease him a tiny bit.

"Watch it with Sharon, okay?"

"Quinn…"

"Please. You need to see this. That girl made a mistake, and you don't deserve to spend the rest of your life afraid of a teenage error in judgment. Watch it; you'll understand."

He tried to be calm but heard the desperation in his own voice.

And he couldn't tell if he'd got through. Her head kept shaking. It didn't look like she was telling him no, more like she couldn't accept what she was hearing. It didn't jibe with what she thought she knew, so disbelief rattled her.

"If he tried to sell that video to any news organization, he would be lynched. He was an adult, which is a crime. It wouldn't matter if you'd been old enough in *hours*. Legally, he'd be screwed if he tried to show that video to anyone."

At this point, he wasn't sure she was hearing him. She didn't answer, but she had stopped shaking her head and seemed more together than he had been most of the night.

It felt as if he should stay with her, but he had to give her time to work through this and still squeeze in a trip down the aisle.

Which brought him to the last bit… The scariest bit.

"One more thing." His hands shook, so he stuffed them into his pockets, then thought better of that and hung his arms at his sides as still and casual as he could, but no amount of trying to slow his breathing would work. "I'm not calling off the wedding. I can't picture my life any other way than with you in it. If you come to the church on Saturday, I plan on making that life we'll share amazing. I'll always fight for you and for us, but I need you to fight too."

She looked at him again, still listening. "I don't understand."

"I'm leaving here and I'm going to talk to the press to make sure they don't blame you for this if you watch that video and decide you still can't be there. I'll do whatever I can to help you stay in the country, or go wherever you want to go if that's your decision."

His finger seemed to throb where the ring sat, the thing that had bolstered him through this. Quietly, he pulled it from his finger and placed it gently atop the divorce papers on her desk, framing her decision with two opposite choices.

With everything he'd thrown at her, there was no way for her to come to any decision right now. If she did, it'd still be *No* without watching the video, and she needed space to do that.

Quinn kissed her forehead, repeated the date, time and location of the wedding for her, asked she watch the video one more time and excused himself while his legs still held him.

All he could do now was wait. And pray...

Quinn had been gone for over an hour when Anais heard Mom gently tapping on her bedroom door.

"I'm okay," she called, hoping it was enough to get a little more quiet alone time to make sense of the things Quinn had said.

The one thing, mostly.

Signing the papers was an act of love. The rest of it... some kind of faith she couldn't even process.

On some level, she knew it was the kind of thing people—especially stupid people like her—would live their entire lives waiting to hear. The kind of words that should bring relief. But she felt nothing. Not even happy to know he hadn't been lying about the depth of his love.

How could she feel happy about that now?

Numb was at least okay enough to not be actively falling apart like she'd been all night.

"Did he take the papers to submit to court?" Still through the door.

The papers. From where she sat on the edge of the bed, she could only focus on that beautiful ring sitting on top of something so ugly.

"He left it up to me," she answered, then the door opened. With a deep, fortifying breath, she added, "I don't want you to worry about this. Stress kicks you out of rhythm, and I'm going to be fine. You don't need to worry."

"You don't look fine, baby girl. You have no color in your face, and you look like you've just witnessed a public execution."

Watch the video with Mom, he'd said. As if she could bear anyone else she loved to know such things, let alone witness them. Drinking. Making out. Nudity. Then the best part, where she smashed Ratliffe's face up with a bottle of cheap rum.

All that was her burden to bear. Consequences for bad judgment and immaturity. Life had handed her a lesson—or she'd grabbed it with both hands—and she'd learned from it.

"Sometimes I wish I'd never met him. Then I wouldn't have had to leave him, hurt him… Hurt me." The words came out and the numbness left in a blink. "But then maybe I'd be someone worse if things had gone another way. Or I guess maybe I'd be someone better too."

"Worse implies that you're bad now. You're not." Mom came fully inside and used the apron she wore to wipe the tears from Anais's cheeks.

"I feel like I am."

"What did Quinton say?"

She shook her head, sifting words for the ones she could share. "That he still wants me, but he won't force me because he needs me to fight for us too. I just don't think there can be a peaceful ride off into the sunset with him. There's just riding, and more riding, and no end to the riding. I'm not strong enough for this."

Quinn's summary didn't match what had happened, and the parts that did match weren't parts that made it any less shameful, pathetic, or stupid.

"You're strong when you need to be. We both are. We'll get through this, whatever you decide."

Support. The last thing she deserved. The trouble was she didn't know what the least selfish thing for her to do was. "I need to sleep. It's after ten a.m.; that's close enough to nap time."

If she gave up her alcohol abstinence, maybe she could sleep her way through the wedding day he refused to cancel.

CHAPTER THIRTEEN

Cocooned from the world, Anais passed the rest of the day and night alternating between sleep and staring at the small drive Quinn had left.

Morning came again, as it always did, and she considered ordering alcohol because now she missed the numbness she'd had in that first hour. Anything was better than this cycle of self-loathing and skepticism.

A knock at her door summoned her out of bed. A short conversation with Mom later, and Anais found herself on the sofa downstairs.

"I waited a whole day, and now you have to watch this."

"What is it?" Anais asked, focusing on the television.

Please God, not the video.

It wasn't. Whatever Mom had recorded started to play and she saw him. Quinn, but this time not in the formal attire he'd worn for his last press conference. He looked much as he'd done yesterday standing in her bedroom, making claims about the video that didn't stack up with the facts she knew to be as true as his hollow, haggard expression.

It hurt to see him. Would always hurt to see him but, after a while—a long while—it could scar over. It had last time. Kind of. It had become older pain, which was at least something peaceful. Something better than this place where her ribs felt as if they were broken and unable to generate the suction required to draw her next breath.

"Can you just summarize it for me? I can't watch him…"

Her broken sob stopped the words. The television clicked off and Mom laid her hand gently on Anais's head, then started smoothing her hair.

"He said, with the way things went for you during your marriage before—being attacked all the time in the media, and disparaged as not good enough for him—you're getting more and more afraid it will go back to that after the wedding."

Gritting her teeth, Anais tried to turn off her emotions again, but all she managed was to wring her hands until the skin burned, and slow, quiet tears.

"Okay," she said, but she still couldn't see how that would make things better. Maybe he was shifting the blame onto the press?

"And you might not be able to make that leap again. That you're afraid of your babies inheriting this stigma, but you haven't made up your mind yet. You're going to take all the time up to the wedding to decide, he said."

"That's not totally true," she said, needing Mom to know the truth, even if she couldn't tell anyone else. "But I guess I didn't say no when he pitched it. I didn't say much of anything."

Mom nodded, but in the morning light she didn't look as frail to Anais as she had since coming home. She looked like that woman who'd worked three jobs so they would stay afloat, refusing to let Anais get a job that would take her away from her studies and the better life Mom had wanted for her. Or maybe that was just what Anais needed her to be right now when her own strength was flagging.

"They're taking some of the blame for it."

"Who?"

"Everyone, I guess. People. Reporters. This morning, woven wedding crowns began appearing on the steps of the cathedral."

"Flowers?"

Mom nodded.

"I guess they really enjoyed The Sip." None of it made sense, especially the hope she felt fluttering in her belly.

"There's something you're not telling me, baby."

Yes.

She didn't want to lie to Mom. "I'm still trying to sort everything out."

"You know he's going to be dressed and at the wedding. People are still attending. It's not cancelled."

Breathe.

If things were as Mom reported, then he'd done what he'd promised—deflected blame. At least enough that she might be able to keep her home. Maybe even enough to work at Almsford again in a few months when the news died down.

There it was again, a lifting feeling that terrified her, that just left her with further to fall.

To hear Quinn talk, she'd been a victim, but really, she'd been stupid—the one thing she'd always had to cling to, cancelling the other things said about her, had been her intellect. But she'd been so stupid that night. Willfully stupid, not just naïve. Stupid and so hungry for attention and any small sense of belonging she'd drank his booze, and did other things.

Made terrible decisions. Got naked. Took photos. Made out. Blacked out...all with a man she wasn't even really attracted to.

None of that matched up with Quinn's victim hypothesis.

Then resolved it all with violence because she wasn't smart enough to handle things civilly.

The day before the wedding, her wedding dress, underthings and accessories came by courier in the morning.

At noon, a van and security men with a hand truck carrying a small safe arrived. The inventory listed the contents: tiara, necklace, earrings, worn by Lady Evelyn in her wedding to Prince Thomas in 1954.

A man with a large bouquet of flowers arrived as the jewelry delivery men left—but a small security detail stayed to provide security overnight.

Anais let them all in, because what else was she supposed to do? Just stood there, being an observer to her life because both choices paralyzed her.

She waved the flowers in, thanked the man, then spent some time staring at the roses, lilies and violets. Nestled in the blooms was a small envelope. A card.

She couldn't bring herself to look at the jewelry in the safe, but she fumbled the card out of the envelope and read Quinn's strong script:

Today's courage is tomorrow's JOY.

The words on her tattoo, but with Quinn's correction.

It struck her like a body blow, the simple word replacement. As did the words tucked beneath:

Watch the video. Please.

He thought she was aiming too low.

"What's it say?" Mom asked, coming down the stairs from her shower.

Anais handed the card over and took the bouquet to her refrigerator to spare the blossoms.

"What video?" Mom asked, following.

Deep breath.

"I need to tell you something."

Saturday morning broke bright and sunny after three days of rain and time that had crawled, maybe even stood still for black stretches of night, when Quinn struggled hardest.

Philip had to practically put him under palace arrest to

keep him from going to Anais's house, especially as days stacked up without word from her.

Now he stood at the altar in the beautifully decorated Romanesque cathedral where all the important family events had happened for centuries, wearing his finest, most stately regalia. And sweating buckets.

Every breath came with effort—not just for him. The entire congregation seemed to hold its breath at the slightest sound from the street beyond the ornately carved—and closed—doors at the far end of the nave.

He watched the door; everyone else watched him.

The place reeked of sweat and flowers, and he couldn't bear to look anyone in the eye for fear he'd see pity there, the certainty she wouldn't come. He especially avoided Philip's eye, and the King—who'd managed to come to the wedding and now sat in the first row.

Everyone who mattered to him was there except her.

She still had a few minutes. She'd come. He had to hold on to that if he wanted to keep from collapsing under the weight of his own decisions.

Ben, his best man, sat in his chair to his left.

Rosalie, who'd agreed to be Anais's maid of honor, waited alone on the bride's side of the altar.

It just wasn't enough time for her to work through it.

He should've postponed the wedding. Or stayed, watched with her, ignored her objections. Made her watch it.

The only thing three days had been enough for was to pull everyone else as far into his worry as he was.

It had been days of him seeing that same brave but stricken expression on every face, including the people lining the street outside the cathedral, waiting. So many clustered at the doors it might be hard for her to make it inside if...*when* she did come.

As if summoned under the weight of his stare and thoughts, the doors rattled and his heart, hammering hard enough to mold steel, fell into his shoes.

In unison, all the heads turned to the door. Breathless seconds passed.

Nothing.

Should he go check?

Could the doors have become locked somehow?

God, please...

His clenched gut answered him.

As coolly as he could, Quinn left the altar and jogged the length of the nave. When the doors opened enough to clear the frame, he closed them again.

Not locked.

She wasn't trying to get in.

She wasn't there.

Right.

He blew out a heavy breath and turned to walk, shoulders square with effort, head high with more effort, back to the altar.

Don't look at the clock.

His wrist felt heavy with the timepiece there. Everything felt heavy.

Everything to do with Anais was a gamble, not just whether or not she'd arrive—he was hanging by a slender thread of hope there—but whether she'd have the press after her and for how long if she didn't.

Should he still offer to renounce for her so they could leave the country together? Could he really abandon Philip to all this? Could he walk away from the last weeks or months he might have with Grandfather?

Yes.

He closed his eyes. Not even sure whether to be ashamed of that.

Anais's side of the cathedral was, ironically, the most packed. Everyone wanted to be seated as her guest, as if their bums on the pews could pull her in. Someone in the back was crying.

Sharon wasn't there either. Which should probably tell him something.

The doors rattled again.

God help him. He wouldn't go check.

He closed his eyes and forced his hands to unclench. His belly moved in and out, proof he was still breathing.

Doors again.

It wasn't until he heard the gasps that his eyes flew open.

She stood at the end of the nave, beautiful in her white dress, those strawberry waves flowing down her back, a bouquet dangling from her left hand.

Shaking, he gave up every pretext of keeping his composure. Some strangled sound of dismay and elation erupted from him.

The music started and she began walking to him.

He was supposed to wait.

The thought barely died before a more forceful one overrode it. To hell with propriety and tradition.

He *sprinted* down the center aisle to her.

"I'm sorry." She got exactly two words out before Quinn grabbed her by her wet cheeks and dragged her mouth to his.

He didn't need words. He only needed her. Her soft lips, her warmth, her grumpy mornings, her ravenous nights.

The kiss filled his chest after endless empty days.

She kissed him back with a frantic heat, grabbing at him—his waist, his hips, then his head, smashing flowers into his hair in desperation to get closer. Full of promises he didn't need spoken, echoing the explanations he didn't need.

Cheering started at some point, and he became aware that it had evolved to giggles and good-natured ribbing, but her arms around his neck and the flowers now smashing into both their faces hid tears he couldn't find a drop of shame for shedding.

"Prince Quinton."

The King's voice broke through and he pulled back from the kiss. They were supposed to get married now.

Her hands slid to his lapels and fisted there, not letting him go before she could whisper in his ear, the three words he'd already heard in her heart weeks ago, but which sounded more beautiful than anything he'd ever heard.

"I love you too." He looked deep into those blue-green eyes he loved, and though they were filled with happiness, hope, and regret, tears streamed down her cheeks.

"Forgive me?" she whispered again.

"After the wedding," he teased, too full of joy to care. On a whim, and because he couldn't even bear the idea of her being inches away from him after days of torture, he swept her up in his arms to carry her toward the altar.

People clapped again, but he had a mission to complete, and refused to put her back on her feet when they reached the priest.

Anais dropped the bouquet in her lap so she could have both her arms around his shoulders, and he didn't hear a word the priest said. All he heard was her, the promises in her eyes, and the future.

He let her down for the ring exchange, and their first official kiss that could've lasted forever as far as Quinn was concerned.

When Philip pelted them with rice ahead of schedule, Quinn reluctantly separated from his wife's sweet lips.

Her fingers stroked through the hair at the back of his head and the smile she gave him… He could finally breathe.

In the aftermath of the video, he knew there were still dark places they'd have to explore together, but if they hadn't stopped her from coming today he wouldn't let anything else stop them from taking those obstacles together. Fighting for each other, never against.

Today's courage for tomorrow's joy.

EPILOGUE

Fifteen months later...

Anais held Pippa, her six-month-old daughter, to her chest as she stood beside King Philip behind a wide red ribbon spanning the entrance of Hero's Welcome, the project she and Quinn had dreamed up on their honeymoon and spent the months since building.

"Daddy and Be-Be are in trouble..." Anais murmured in sing-song fashion to Pippa and Philip, scanning the road behind them for signs of movement before she turned back to the crowd of citizens, soldiers and cameras there for the opening.

Life was so good she could hardly believe it from day to day, sometimes minute to minute. Even when her husband was late for their big dedication day.

"Where are they?" Philip muttered through his dutiful smiles.

"School..." Anais started to answer, but then she heard running behind her and turned to see Quinn and Ben Nettle racing toward them.

Even when irritated with him, her heart never failed to beat faster when she saw him.

"Sorry," Quinn panted, kissed her cheek, and then reached for his daughter. "Test ran late."

Pippa went eagerly into Quinn's arms, and Anais couldn't

blame her. Hands free, she fetched the oversized ceremo-
nial scissors for Corrachlean's Bachelor King to use, if the
autumn sky held back the rain until he'd finished the dedication speech.

Ben joined a pregnant Rosalie on the other side of the
ribbon, still using his chair on university days. He'd gotten steady enough with both prosthetics to walk her back
down the aisle last month, but it was still work for him to
move around for long periods on them. He'd get there and,
in the meanwhile, he and Quinn tackled university together.

Rejoining her perfect little family, Anais tucked in
close to Quinn as Philip went over the assets of Hero's
Welcome—the country's first specialized community for
wounded veterans to assist them in readjusting to private
life with their new challenges.

"How did you do?" she whispered to Quinn while Pippa
alternated between shoving her fist into her own mouth and
shoving into Daddy's.

"Goog…" he garbled around the slobbery baby fist, then
pulled it from his mouth and made faces at her to keep their
strong-willed baby from making her displeasure known
about formal duties.

"Show me your grade later, and I'll give you a reward,"
she cooed in his ear. The man was a terrible influence on
her, tempting her to goof off and flirt with him at their big
opening.

Philip, who'd ascended about four months after the wedding, didn't mind so much when they goofed around. He
was still getting used to the position, which he'd inherited
unexpectedly when King Thomas, after a couple of months
of relatively good health, didn't wake one morning.

"Dr. Anais Corlow will be operating the community
clinic."

She stopped quietly misbehaving when she heard her
name and waved briefly, smiling. Philip had stopped calling her *Princess* in favor of Doctor at her request, even if

she was technically stuck with the title until Philip married and produced an heir. Something he'd better get on with if he didn't want her to start funneling women in his direction.

After talking about the clinic, Philip went down the list.

Mrs. Rosalie Nettle—Job Center Administrator
Lieutenant Benjamin Nettle—Counselor.

"Prince Quinton Corlow…in charge of making faces to amuse Princess Pippa, until he graduates, and then something with physical therapy."

Quinn had the grace to look fleetingly chagrined at his introduction, but rebounded with a quick smile.

He'd be a great part-time PT. He had other jobs that came first: devoted husband, delighted daddy, and sometimes reluctant but ever-faithful diplomat.

Philip left off the names of the operators for the community's amenities. Aunt Helen at the salon, Mom at the community center, and those operating the market, butcher, bakery, pharmacy, bank, and post office. But they had it all, a fully functioning community.

Philip cut the ribbon and, after the applause and photos, Quinn stopped goofing around with Pippa long enough to announce, "There's food and drink at the community center, and several of the differently equipped cottages are available for tours. Finally, Princess Pippa has graciously made herself available to drool on anyone who gets too close. At the community center. We're following the food."

He made her laugh every day. He never wavered when she got overwhelmed by some aspect of royal life, which blessedly was happening with less frequency.

She'd never felt she truly belonged anywhere, so they'd built a place where she unquestioningly belonged. They'd sold the penthouse and the townhouse, and built their new home within the community.

Wayne wasn't even a ghost on her horizon anymore. The

longer she spent with her new family, the better life got, and the less Wayne Ratliffe mattered at all.

Her family and her purpose gave her the kind of peace that came in second to the joy of Quinn's morning wake-up attacks, and Pippa's strawberry curls and stormy gray eyes.

* * * * *

If you enjoyed this story, check out these other great reads from Amalie Berlin

DANTE'S SHOCK PROPOSAL
CHALLENGING THE DOCTOR SHEIKH
TAMING HOLLYWOOD'S ULTIMATE PLAYBOY
FALLING FOR HER RELUCTANT SHEIKH

All available now!

MILLS & BOON®
Hardback – September 2017

ROMANCE

The Tycoon's Outrageous Proposal	Miranda Lee
Cipriani's Innocent Captive	Cathy Williams
Claiming His One-Night Baby	Michelle Smart
At the Ruthless Billionaire's Command	Carole Mortimer
Engaged for Her Enemy's Heir	Kate Hewitt
His Drakon Runaway Bride	Tara Pammi
The Throne He Must Take	Chantelle Shaw
The Italian's Virgin Acquisition	Michelle Conder
A Proposal from the Crown Prince	Jessica Gilmore
Sarah and the Secret Sheikh	Michelle Douglas
Conveniently Engaged to the Boss	Ellie Darkins
Her New York Billionaire	Andrea Bolter
The Doctor's Forbidden Temptation	Tina Beckett
From Passion to Pregnancy	Tina Beckett
The Midwife's Longed-For Baby	Caroline Anderson
One Night That Changed Her Life	Emily Forbes
The Prince's Cinderella Bride	Amalie Berlin
Bride for the Single Dad	Jennifer Taylor
A Family for the Billionaire	Dani Wade
Taking Home the Tycoon	Catherine Mann

0817 GEN STD HB

MILLS & BOON®
Large Print – September 2017

ROMANCE

The Sheikh's Bought Wife	Sharon Kendrick
The Innocent's Shameful Secret	Sara Craven
The Magnate's Tempestuous Marriage	Miranda Lee
The Forced Bride of Alazar	Kate Hewitt
Bound by the Sultan's Baby	Carol Marinelli
Blackmailed Down the Aisle	Louise Fuller
Di Marcello's Secret Son	Rachael Thomas
Conveniently Wed to the Greek	Kandy Shepherd
His Shy Cinderella	Kate Hardy
Falling for the Rebel Princess	Ellie Darkins
Claimed by the Wealthy Magnate	Nina Milne

HISTORICAL

The Secret Marriage Pact	Georgie Lee
A Warriner to Protect Her	Virginia Heath
Claiming His Defiant Miss	Bronwyn Scott
Rumours at Court (Rumors at Court)	Blythe Gifford
The Duke's Unexpected Bride	Lara Temple

MEDICAL

Their Secret Royal Baby	Carol Marinelli
Her Hot Highland Doc	Annie O'Neil
His Pregnant Royal Bride	Amy Ruttan
Baby Surprise for the Doctor Prince	Robin Gianna
Resisting Her Army Doc Rival	Sue MacKay
A Month to Marry the Midwife	Fiona McArthur

MILLS & BOON®
Hardback – October 2017

ROMANCE

Claimed for the Leonelli Legacy	Lynne Graham
The Italian's Pregnant Prisoner	Maisey Yates
Buying His Bride of Convenience	Michelle Smart
The Tycoon's Marriage Deal	Melanie Milburne
Undone by the Billionaire Duke	Caitlin Crews
His Majesty's Temporary Bride	Annie West
Bound by the Millionaire's Ring	Dani Collins
The Virgin's Shock Baby	Heidi Rice
Whisked Away by Her Sicilian Boss	Rebecca Winters
The Sheikh's Pregnant Bride	Jessica Gilmore
A Proposal from the Italian Count	Lucy Gordon
Claiming His Secret Royal Heir	Nina Milne
Sleigh Ride with the Single Dad	Alison Roberts
A Firefighter in Her Stocking	Janice Lynn
A Christmas Miracle	Amy Andrews
Reunited with Her Surgeon Prince	Marion Lennox
Falling for Her Fake Fiancé	Sue MacKay
The Family She's Longed For	Lucy Clark
Billionaire Boss, Holiday Baby	Janice Maynard
Billionaire's Baby Bind	Katherine Garbera

MILLS & BOON®
Large Print – October 2017

ROMANCE

Sold for the Greek's Heir	Lynne Graham
The Prince's Captive Virgin	Maisey Yates
The Secret Sanchez Heir	Cathy Williams
The Prince's Nine-Month Scandal	Caitlin Crews
Her Sinful Secret	Jane Porter
The Drakon Baby Bargain	Tara Pammi
Xenakis's Convenient Bride	Dani Collins
Her Pregnancy Bombshell	Liz Fielding
Married for His Secret Heir	Jennifer Faye
Behind the Billionaire's Guarded Heart	Leah Ashton
A Marriage Worth Saving	Therese Beharrie

HISTORICAL

The Debutante's Daring Proposal	Annie Burrows
The Convenient Felstone Marriage	Jenni Fletcher
An Unexpected Countess	Laurie Benson
Claiming His Highland Bride	Terri Brisbin
Marrying the Rebellious Miss	Bronwyn Scott

MEDICAL

Their One Night Baby	Carol Marinelli
Forbidden to the Playboy Surgeon	Fiona Lowe
A Mother to Make a Family	Emily Forbes
The Nurse's Baby Secret	Janice Lynn
The Boss Who Stole Her Heart	Jennifer Taylor
Reunited by Their Pregnancy Surprise	Louisa Heaton

MILLS & BOON®

Why shop at millsandboon.co.uk?

Each year, thousands of romance readers find their perfect read at millsandboon.co.uk. That's because we're passionate about bringing you the very best romantic fiction. Here are some of the advantages of shopping at www.millsandboon.co.uk:

* **Get new books first**—you'll be able to buy your favourite books one month before they hit the shops

* **Get exclusive discounts**—you'll also be able to buy our specially created monthly collections, with up to 50% off the RRP

* **Find your favourite authors**—latest news, interviews and new releases for all your favourite authors and series on our website, plus ideas for what to try next

* **Join in**—once you've bought your favourite books, don't forget to register with us to rate, review and join in the discussions

Visit **www.millsandboon.co.uk**
for all this and more today!